On the Wagon

From the Tales of Dan Coast

On the Wagon

From the Tales of Dan Coast

By

Rodney Riesel

Published by Island Holiday Publishing
East Greenbush, NY

Special thanks to:

Pamela Guerriere

Kevin Cook

Cover Design by:

Connie Fitsik

To learn about my other books friend me at

https://www.facebook.com/rodneyriesel

For Brenda,
Kayleigh, Ethan
& Peyton

Chapter One

Red Baxter glanced down at his speedometer. He was doing seventy-five and heading south on US1. The sun had set but the cloudless sky was still blue with a little orange and purple on the horizon. The mile marker signs were rapidly counting down and he had reached number seven. He looked over at a road sign as he passed it that read, SLOWER TRAFFIC KEEP RIGHT.

"Right lane, asshole!" Red shouted as he yanked the wheel hard left, entering the median and sending two orange traffic cones hurtling skyward.

"Language," Dan said from the passenger seat. "Little ears." He pointed into the backseat and then looked over his shoulder at the six-year-old girl lying in the backseat. He smiled. "We'll have you home in no time, sweetheart." The child returned a nervous grin. Dan raised his eyes and stared out the rear window at the two vehicles in pursuit—a brown, late model Buick Electra and a black, newer model Ford F-150.

The young passenger with dark hair and light brown skin was Elisa Pena. She was wearing the same blue and white checkered dress she was wearing a week earlier, when she was abducted on her way home from school. It was the same dress as the one in the photographs that had been plastered all over the local TV news and newspapers, and stapled to telephone poles for the last week.

Red was now in the northbound lane and one oncoming car after the other was swerving out of his way. Tires and brakes squealed and screeched around them.

"Get back in the other lane!" Dan hollered.

"No one likes a backseat driver," Red replied.

"No one likes a dead one either."

Elisa's head peeked over the seat to get a look out the front window.

"Lay back down, honey," Dan told her.

Red veered back into the southbound lane. "There. Are ya happy?" he asked.

"I'll be happier when we reach the police station," Dan responded.

"You better call Rick and let him know we're coming in hot."

Dan looked over at the big man dressed in blue jeans and a red Hawaiian shirt. "Coming in hot?" he asked. "Where the hell did that come from?"

Red grinned. "Yeah, I knew I shouldn't have said it the minute it left my mouth."

Dan pulled his cell phone from one of the pockets in his cargo shorts. "Coming in hot," he repeated as he dialed the phone. "What's next, Ah-nuld? Get to de choppah!"

"Oh, shut up, ya dick."

"Language."

"Hello?" Rick Carver answered.

"What's up, buddy?" Dan asked, with sarcastic glee.

A shot rang out and Red's rear window shattered. Elisa shrieked and curled herself into a fetal ball. Dan reached out a comforting hand even as his pulse clanged in his eardrums.

"What the hell was that noise?" Rick asked.

"That was the sound of Red's window being shot out by some angry Latinos," said Dan. "Can I say Latinos? That's not racist, is it?"

"Where are you?"

"We're on US1 coming into Key West. Are you at the station?"

"Yes."

"We'll be there in a few minutes. We're being chased by a brown Buick and a black Ford pick-up. We have Elisa Pena with us."

"Elisa Pena? How ... what—"

"I'll explain it all when we get there. Oh, and Rick."

"Yeah?"

"We're coming in hot."

Red shook his head. "You couldn't just let it go, could ya?"

Dan hung up the cell and watched out the broken glass as the Buick closed the gap between them. An arm holding a 9mm came out of the passenger side window of the pick-up. Dan saw the barrel flash twice but heard no sound. "Step on it!" he urged.

"Step on it?" Red repeated. "Like that's not just as bad as *coming in hot*."

"I don't think it is," Dan shot back. "Everyone says 'step on it.'"

"Whatever."

Red hit the brakes and slid around the corner onto North Roosevelt Drive. "They still with us?" he asked.

"Yut. The stupid bastards are gonna follow us right to the police station."

The Buick followed Red around the corner but the Ford took a left.

"I want my mommy," Elisa quietly said.

"I know you do, princess," Dan responded. "Don't worry, we won't let the bad guys get you."

The passenger in the Buick fired off another round, hitting the roof of Red's car.

Red glanced down at the 9mm in his friend's hand. "Shoot back for chrissakes!" Red hollered.

"I'm not firing a gun out of a moving vehicle. It's too dangerous," Dan shouted back.

"Someone should have explained that to them," Red said, throwing a thumb over his shoulder. He rounded the bend in front of IHOP and could see flashing lights coming toward them. "Thank God, it's the calvary."

"Cavalry," said Dan.

"That's what I said."

"You said calvary."

"What's the dif—"

The Ford shot out of Glynn Archer Drive, crashing into the front, driver's side fender of Red's Firebird and spinning the car like a child's top. Red struggled with the steering wheel to right the car.

The pickup hit its breaks and slid across the street, jumped the curb, and slammed into a utility pole. Smoke gushed from underneath the mangled hood as the truck's horn bleated a single angry note. The driver was slumped over the steering wheel, either dead or unconscious. Dan rooted for dead.

Red's stalled Firebird was sitting in the street facing back the way they had come. Elisa was lying on the floor, screaming. "It's all right, princess," Dan whispered. "We've got the bad guys on the run." *I wish.* He tried to open his door; it was jammed. "Red, stay here with Elisa." Before Red could protest Dan grabbed his gun from the floorboard and climbed out the window.

The Buick skidded to a stop sideways in the street, the driver's side facing Dan and Red. The passenger jumped from the car and began firing his AK-47 as he walked toward the incapacitated Firebird. Bullets sprayed the front bumper, hood, and windshield. Dan took cover at the rear of the vehicle.

"Jesus, we're sitting ducks," Red muttered, raking shards of glass off his lap. "Come on, darlin'." He reached into the backseat, scooping up the young girl with one hand as he opened his door. He pulled her to his beefy chest, shielding her from the flying bullets, and ran to join Dan.

Dan fired over the roof of the car, hitting the driver in the leg. "Red, you crazy bastard, I thought I told you to stay put!"

Red was hunched over on his knees with Elisa beneath him. "What, and let you have all the fun?"

The passenger kept firing.

Dan looked over his shoulder at the Ford pickup; he saw movement behind the steering wheel. *Shit!* He thought. The goddamn driver was still alive after all.

Two Key West police cruisers came to a halt fifty yards behind them, lights flashing and sirens wailing. The officers jumped from their vehicles and took cover behind the open doors of their cars.

Dan stood and stepped out from behind Red's car and began firing his weapon as fast as he could pull the trigger. His third shot hit the passenger in the shoulder and his fifth hit him in the chest.

The passenger stumbled backwards and fell on his back, where he lay motionless.

Dan turned his weapon on the driver. The round ricocheted off the blacktop and hit him in the other leg. The driver screamed out in pain.

The driver of the pickup exited his vehicle and pointed his weapon at Dan. Dan stepped in front of Red and the young girl. Dan pulled his trigger. Nothing. The magazine was spent.

Dan closed his eyes. A shot rang out and Dan flinched. He opened one eye and then the other. The driver lay dead in the street. Dan looked to his left to see Rick Carver aiming his .357 over the hood of his cruiser.

Two other officers ran to the driver of the Buick and cuffed his hands behind his back. Rick walked toward Dan and Red. When he was almost to them Dan leaned forward and threw up.

Rick stepped back to avoid the splash. Stepping over the fresh pile, he walked up to Dan. Rick sniffed the air. Besides the puke, he could smell alcohol. "Are you drunk?" he asked.

"I've had a few," Dan replied. "I wasn't driving though. He was."

Rick turned to Red. "Have you been drinking, you idiot?"

"Not a drop," Red said. "I'm not *that* stupid."

"Yeah, you are," Rick argued.

More cruisers pulled up and other officers swarmed the area. Some kept back the onlookers and others began directing traffic.

Dan and Red looked at each other and grinned. Red nudged the little girl toward Rick. "There ya go, princess," he said. "See, I told ya, everything is gonna be okay."

Elisa wiped the tears from her eyes. "Gracias," she whispered.

"De nada," Red replied.

Dan looked around at all the commotion and then slapped his old pal on the back. "Come on, amigo, I need a drink."

Rick stopped Dan in his tracks with a palm to the chest. "Not so fast, ya goddamn drunk. I think you two better come with me down to the station and answer a few questions."

"I think it's you who needs to answer a question," Dan informed him.

"Oh yeah? What question would that be?"

Dan gave Rick a condescending smirk. "Like, what would this town do without us?"

Rick's face quickly reddened and he pointed his finger back at his police cruiser. "Get in the car!"

Chapter Two

Rick Carver's police cruiser pulled up in front of the white beach bungalow with green trim at 632 Beach View Street. The passenger side door swung open and out climbed Dan Coast.

"Thanks for the ride, Rick," he said.

Rick didn't answer.

Dan shut the door and turned toward his house. As he walked up the path that led to the front door he paused and looked over at the used 2012 Porsche 911 S Cabriolet. The black beauty was a nice replacement for the one he had crashed into a block wall the day after Christmas over two years ago. Dan purchased the car in Miami—a steal at only $58,000. Mint condition, the ad said, but there was a small ding in the driver's side door where some shit wad had hit it with a shopping cart or something.

Dan walked over to the fine piece of German engineering, opened the door, and climbed in. He made himself comfortable in the brown leather seat. He adjusted the rear view mirror so he could see himself. There was a small cut above his left eye from a scuffle that took place before the mornings car chase. There were bags under his eyes and three deep wrinkles across his forehead. He slapped the mirror away and reached under the seat for the bottle of tequila awaiting him.

Unscrewing the cap, he took a big swig, replaced the cap, and slid the bottle back under the seat. He put the seat back a ways and stared up at the dark starry sky. The palm fronds of the tree next to the driveway swayed in the breeze above his head. He drifted off.

*****

"Dan!" Maxine called out from the front steps. "Da-*an!*"

"Alex?" Dan whispered quietly and opened his eyes.

"What are you doing?" Maxine asked.

Dan raised the seat. "Nothing. Just sitting here." He stretched his arms over his head. "What's the matter?"

"Nothing. I thought I heard a car door shut and I looked out and saw you sleeping there." Maxine walked down the steps toward her boyfriend.

"How long have I been out here?" Dan asked.

"Three minutes, maybe."

"Oh." Dan opened the door and climbed out. He glanced across the street to see Edna McGee, his eighty-something neighbor across the street, staring out her front window. Dan ignored her.

"Have you been drinking?" Maxine asked.

Dan walked past her toward the front door. "Jesus Christ! Why does everyone keep asking me that? It's a stupid question. Chances are I've been drinking, Maxine." He walked up the steps through the screened in porch, and stepped over the doormat that read THE COASTS.

Maxine followed him into the house. She sat on the couch with the palm tree print. A repeat of Dr. Phil was on the Oprah Winfrey Network, and Phil was telling someone they were full of shit. The guy receiving the lecture already knew he was full of shit, but he hoped he could slide it by Dr. Phil without him knowing. He couldn't. No one ever could. If the good doc had said it once, he had said it a thousand times: you can put feathers on a dog, but that don't make it a chicken.

Maxine listened as Dan went into the kitchen and poured himself a glass of water. He drank half the glass and poured the rest into the sink.

Dan walked through the dining room and into the living room without looking at Maxine. Then he entered the hallway, went into the bathroom, and closed the door behind him.

Maxine glanced over at Buddy, who was lying on his flannel bed next to the small table that held a framed picture of Dan's deceased wife, Alex. The aging dog opened one eye as though he knew he was being stared at. Maxine's eyes went back to the TV.

Ten minutes past and the toilet flushed. The bathroom door opened, and Dan walked back into the living room. "I've got to quit drinking," he said.

"Okay," Maxine answered.

"I mean, I drink way too much."

"Yes."

"But I don't want to stop drinking."

"That's a problem."

"Do you think everyone thinks I'm a drunk?"

"I think everyone thinks you drink too much."

"Do *you* think I'm a drunk?"

"I think you *drink* way too much."

"How does someone stop drinking if they don't want to stop drinking? I don't want to stop drinking, Maxine. I love to drink."

"They have progra—"

"I'm not doing that. I'm not gonna stand in a room full of losers and tell them all that I'm a loser too."

"They're not losers … and neither are you."

Dan took in a deep breath and sighed. "Maybe not, but I can't do it." He walked around the dining room table to the bar, grabbed a rocks glass, and went to the freezer to fill it with ice. When he returned he poured himself a shot of tequila and topped it off with 7UP. When he turned around he caught Maxine's stare. "I'll start tomorrow," he said.

Chapter Three

It was 6:10 the next morning—Wednesday morning—and Dan stood at the foot of his bed pulling on a light gray, long-sleeved T-shirt. On the front of the shirt, in black lettering, it said Property of Myrtle Beach. He was wearing navy-blue gym shorts. The light was off and only the moonlight lit the room.

"What are you doing?" Maxine asked.

"Gonna try to run again," Dan answered.

Any other morning Maxine would have ribbed him about the idea of a run; she had done it a few times in the past, but after last night's talk she gave a supportive "that's great" you want some company?"

"Maybe tomorrow."

"Okay. I'll make breakfast while you're gone."

"Thanks. That would be great."

Dan turned and left the room. Maxine waited until she heard the door shut and threw back the covers. She walked to the front door in her pajamas and bare feet. She bent to scratch Buddy behind the ears as she went by on her way out the front door. She stepped out onto the steps and watched in the darkness as Dan jogged down the street and around the corner onto George Street. She turned and went back inside.

When Dan returned from his run it was 6:38.

"Two miles?" Maxine called out from the kitchen.

Dan smiled to himself. "I think so," he replied. He looked down at Buddy. "You eat yet?"

"He ate," Maxine said.

"You wanna go outside?"

Buddy jumped up and ran under the dining room table to grab his tennis ball.

Dan held out his hand for the ball, but Buddy ran for the door instead; Dan followed. "Smells good," he said on his way through the kitchen.

"Smoked apple bacon," Maxine informed him.

"Flavored coffee, flavored bacon. What's next, flavored eggs?" He pulled the door shut behind him.

Dan and his best friend walked down the gravel pathway, past the fire pit and two Adirondack chairs, and between the shed and hammock to the beach.

Buddy dropped the tennis ball near the water and froze, looking out over the calm ocean waters. Dan picked up the ball and threw it with all his might into the water; Buddy went after it.

"Here sharky shark, here sharky shark," Dan called out.

Buddy retrieved the ball, brought it back, and dropped it in the wet sand at his master's feet. Dan picked it up and once again threw it as hard as he could. It took five more throws before Buddy was tired and kept the ball to himself. He lay down, and Dan sat Indian style next to him, resting his arm on the mutt's back.

"How's it going, fella?" Dan asked.

Buddy said nothing.

"I don't think *I'm* doing too good."

Buddy laid his head on Dan's knee.

"The booze doesn't seem to be doing what it used to. It's not keeping away the thoughts it used to keep away … or the memories." Dan put his hand under Buddy's chin, turned his head toward him, and looked into the dog's eyes. "I should feel happy, shouldn't I? I have a great girlfriend, a few great friends. Christ, that lottery win gave me more money than—well, you know." He lowered Buddy's head back onto his knee and the two gazed out over the water. "Sometimes I feel like it's just you and me and everyone else is just secondary characters in the story of our life. I don't really feel like they're a part of it. You know what I mean, boy?"

Buddy let out a little sound that was a cross between a grunt and a sigh.

Dan rubbed the dog's head. "Yeah, you know what I mean," he said.

"Breakfast is ready!" Maxine hollered through the screen door.

Dan turned his head toward the house. "Come on, pal, let's get something to eat. Oh, and I was just joking when you jumped in the water and I yelled for the sharks. I love ya, dog. *Don't* tell anyone I said that or I'll cut your nuts off. Ya got it?"

Dan jumped up and the two headed for the back door.

Maxine handed Dan a fresh cup of hot coffee when he came through the door. "Hey, thanks," he said.

Buddy ran past the couple and plopped down on his bed.

Dan blew into the mug.

"What were you two talking about out there?" Maxine asked.

"Hot cars, sexy women, and good cigars. The usual stuff guys talk about," Dan replied, and took a sip of his coffee.

"He's a good dog. Don't be corrupting him with your evil ways."

"What can I say? I'm a bad influence."

"Sit down and I'll bring you your plate."

"Coffee at the door, breakfast delivered. Did I forget it was my birthday or something?"

Maxine turned back toward the stove. "Go sit down, smartass."

Maxine entered the dining room a minute later carrying a plate filled with scrambled eggs, bacon, and toast, expecting to see Dan at the table, but instead he was seated in his recliner with his feet up. "I'll be taking my breakfast in the parlor, Lovey," he said in his best Thurston Howell III impersonation.

Maxine grinned. "Don't push it," she warned.

Chapter Four

Red reached for a rocks glass and the bottle of tequila the second Dan walked through the front door of Red's Bar and Grill.

Dan put up hand. "Just 7UP today, pal," he said.

"What?" Red shouted. "Someone better call hell and see if the schools are closed 'cause me thinks there's a blizzard." He dropped the bottle of tequila back in the well.

"Good one," Dan replied sarcastically. "You write that one yourself?"

"No, I saw it on TV."

"Figures." Dan took a seat on his favorite orange vinyl-covered bar stool. He glanced over at the jukebox from which Jimmy Buffett was singing "Come Monday." The four ceiling fans spun slowly above his head. It was a few minutes after eleven and the lunch crowed hadn't started filing in.

Red sat down the rocks glass and grabbed a soda glass from the shelf behind him.

"Not in one of those glasses, goddammit. Put it in a drink glass."

"Okay, okay. Calm down."

"I'm not a child for chrissakes. Put a lime wedge in there too. I want to at least feel like I'm drinking alcohol."

Red did as he was asked and placed the glass on the bar in front of his pal. "There ya go, little buckaroo."

"Up yours," Dan said and sipped the soda. "Mmm, good."

Red poured himself a cup of coffee. "There was nothing in the paper about us this morning … about us rescuing that kid."

"Probably happened too late in the day. I'm sure there'll be something in there tomorrow, ya glory hound."

"Well, what's the sense in doing a good deed if no one's gonna know about it? I gotta get one of those Facebook pages so I can write about all the good shit I do, like everyone else does."

Dan cocked his head. "What good things have you done?"

Red looked toward the ceiling for an answer. "Umm … I gave that homeless guy a fiver last week," he announced proudly.

"That's great," Dan responded. "And how many *fivers* did you keep for yourself?"

"Hey! I didn't see you give him anything. You just walked by and nodded and said, 'How's it going, bud?'"

"What's wrong with that?"

"How's it *going*, bud? How the hell did you think it was going? He's homeless … he doesn't have a home."

"So you're saying I should have bought him a house?"

"Well, we both know you could afford it."

"How would it have looked if I bought the guy a house and all you gave him was five bucks? You would have looked like a real asshole. I was just thinking of you, pal." Dan slid his empty glass back across the bar. "Fill 'er up."

Red filled the glass. "So, what's next?" he asked.

"Next with what?"

"We got another case?"

"No. *We* don't have another case"

"Oh," said Red disappointedly. "What did Maxine say about yesterday's fiasco?"

"I didn't mention it."

"You didn't mention it!"

"No."

"How do you not mention saving a little girl from kidnappers and going on a high-speed chase that ends in a shootout that leaves two people dead?"

"Wow, it sounds way more exciting when you tell it. Maybe I should have informed all my"—Dan made finger quotes—"Facebook friends."

"Maybe you should have at least informed the woman you live with."

"Naw, that's not a good idea. She gets pissed about things like that. She thinks I'm gonna get hurt."

"You probably will."

"None of my blood was spilled."

"No, just a little puke."

"Don't remind me. Not my proudest moment."

"Don't let it bother ya, pal. Most people on this rock have seen you way worse than that, and doing far dumber things."

"Thanks, Red."

"What are friends for?"

"Sometimes I wonder."

Red took a sip of his coffee. "Ya know, she's gonna be angrier when she finds out on her own. It's like you never learn anything from your mistakes."

"I'm not the relationship expert you are." Dan felt his phone vibrate in his pocket and reached for it. He looked at the caller ID. "Shit! It's Maxine."

Red cringed. "Where is she?" he asked.

Dan stared at the cell. "At work."

"Are ya gonna answer it?"

"I don't want to. She was in a pretty good mood when I dropped her off this morning."

"She's probably not in a good mood anymore."

"Probably not." Dan answered his phone. "What's up, sweetie?" he asked fearfully. "We were just talking about you."

"What happened yesterday?" Maxine asked sternly.

"Did I mention how pretty you looked this morning?"

"What the hell is wrong with you?"

"I guess I'm just a sucker for a woman in scrubs."

Red looked on with a grin.

"Dan!" Maxine scolded.

"Maxine," Dan replied.

The call ended.

"Maxine?"

"What did she say?" Red asked.

"She hung up on me."

"You're *i-in* trou-*ble*," Red sang.

"Well, the good part is, I gave her a ride to work, so she can't leave. So she'll have about"—Dan glanced up at the clock on the wall behind the bar—"ten hours to cool down."

"Or ten hours to let the anger grow inside her."

"Let's hope not." Dan slid his glass back across the bar.

"Tequila?" Red asked.

"No, just 7UP."

"Are ya sure you don't want to be half in the bag when she gets home? Might make the confrontation a little easier."

"I'm sure. Besides, if I got drunk she would have to walk home from work tonight, and you remember what happened the last time she had to do that."

"Of course I remember, it was just last week."

"Oh yeah."

"And a few weeks before that."

"That's enough."

"You would think she would learn."

"Enough."

"I mean, fool me once. Am I right?"

Dan cocked his head to the left. "Ya know, you're right. She is partially to blame."

"So then a tequila?" Red asked.

"Wow, you're like a drug dealer."

Red shrugged. "Only, booze isn't a drug."

"Some people say it is."

"Yeah, stupid people."

"Just a soda," said Dan.

Red grabbed his glass and filled it with ice. "Suit yourself. You want something to eat?"

Dan thought for a second. "Yeah, give me a fish sandwich and fries."

"Comin' right up," Red replied, and disappeared through the kitchen door. "Jocko! Fish sandwich and fries!"

Dan sipped his soda and then his cell phone vibrated again. "Hello?"

"Dan?"

"Yeah."

"It's Rick."

"I know."

"Can you and Red come down to the station this afternoon?"

"What for?"

"We have some more questions for you."

"You already asked us a bunch of questions."

"The mayor and the district attorney have a few questions for you."

"Crap! Are we in trouble? You sound angry."

"Just be here at three." Rick hung up the phone.

Red walked back through the swinging door into the bar.

Dan held up his phone. "Rick just called."

"And?"

"I think we might be in some trouble. He wants us both down to the station at three to answer some questions."

"*More* questions?"

"He said the mayor and the district attorney have a few questions for us."

"Huh," Red said. "What do you think that's all about?"

"We're probably getting sued or something."

"Don't be ridiculous. Who would sue us, the kidnappers?" Red stared silently across the bar at his friend for a few seconds and then a grin flashed across his face. "I bet they're gonna give us a reward."

"You *would* think that," Dan said, shaking his head.

"Think about it, pal. We saved that little girl's life. They're gonna give us a medal. There'll probably be a parade."

"I think you're getting a little carried away."

"Yeah," Red agreed. "Carried away on the shoulders of the townspeople."

"Townspeople? Where do *you* live, Walnut Grove? If anything the *townspeople* will be coming at us with pitchforks and torches."

"Is that a joke about my big head? Are you saying I look like Frankenstein?"

"Frankenstein's monster."

"What?"

"Frankenstein was the mad scientist. You look like Frankenstein's Monster."

"Wow, you don't even have to be drinking to be a dick, do ya?"

"Nope. I can be just as big a dick whether drunk or sober. I'm what the experts call ambi*dicks*trous."

Chapter Five

Dan Coast parked his Porsche in the parking lot of the Key West Police Department. Red jumped from the passenger seat over the door and eagerly made his way toward the building. Dan, not so eagerly, followed along.

Red pulled open the door and with a wave of his arm motioned for his friend to enter first.

Dan grabbed the door and said, "No, you go ahead," and Red did just that.

"Good afternoon, Nancy," Red said with a grin to the woman behind the desk. "How are you today?"

Nancy, the receptionist for the last fifteen years, replied, "Good, Red. You?" Nancy was slightly overweight—big boned, some might say. She had long, dirty blonde hair with pinkish highlights pulled up into a top knot bun that squatted atop her head like a tribble—a tribble impaled by Nancy's well chewed yellow number two pencil. Nancy had an unusually small head and wore black, thick-rimmed glasses that made her look a little like a female Woody Allen.

"So far, so good," Red replied.

Nancy reached under the desk and pushed a button that sounded a buzzer. "They're expecting you."

The buzzing stopped just as Red yanked on the door handle of the plate glass door. It didn't budge.

Dan chuckled.

Nancy pushed the button again and Red pulled the door open.

"Nancy," said Dan on his way through the door.

"Dan," Nancy returned.

The two men walked across the room to the Masonite hollow-core door that read CHIEF OF POLICE, RICHARD CARVER.

Red knocked and entered. "Good afternoon, Richard," he said.

"Have a seat, gentlemen," said a man that stood with authority next to Rick's desk. He wore a gray three piece suit and his arms were folded across his chest. Dan recognized the man as District Attorney Martin Cane.

Standing behind Rick, with his back to the men, and staring out the window, was Mayor Greg Lyndsay. He turned toward them as they sat in the two leather chairs in front of the desk.

Cane cleared his throat and then asked, "So, how did you two know where to find the Pena kid?"

"A friend of ours called Dan and said—"

"Anonymous tip," Dan said, interrupting Red.

Red nodded. "Yeah, it was an anonymous friend of ours." He glanced over at Dan.

Cane looked from Rick to Lyndsay and then back at the dynamic duo. "It'll come out at the trial," he said.

"If you think so," said Dan.

Cane snickered through his nose. "Carver said you were a wise ass."

"If you're good at something, stick with it, I always say," Dan responded.

"We can discuss who the bigger wise ass is at a later date," Mayor Lyndsay said. "What I want to know, Coast, is can you refrain from being a wise ass for an hour or so?"

"If you give me some time to prepare," Dan replied. "I can't just behave at a moment's notice."

Lyndsay chuckled and looked at Red. "He always like this?"

"No," Red said. "Sometimes he's worse."

"The reason they're asking," Rick explained, "is because the city would like to present you two with citations for your part in yesterday's rescue of the Pena girl."

"What the hell!" Red said angrily. "We didn't do anything wrong. We were just trying to help."

"Not that kind of citation, you idiot!" Rick hollered.

"Rick!" Lydsay scolded. "What the chief is trying to say is that we will be honoring the two of you at a ceremony next week. You will each receive a citation and a plaque from the City of Key West."

"Oh," Red said, and then turned to Dan. "See, I told ya. We're heroes." He turned his attention back to the mayor. "Will there be something in tomorrow's newspaper about this, because I looked this morning and there wasn't anything."

"I'm sure there'll be something in the paper," said Cane.

"Good," Red said. "Will there be food and an open bar?"

All three men stared blankly at the moron before them.

"I'll take that as a no," said Red.

After the meeting the men shook hands and Dan and Red returned to Dan's car.

"That's pretty cool," Red said.

"Yeah, pretty cool," Dan repeated.

"Are you being sarcastic?"

"A little."

"Why? I would think this would be perfect for you. How can Maxine be angry with you if the entire city honors you for being a hero?"

Dan pulled open his door and looked over the car at Red. "You do realize you're the only one who used the word hero."

"They were thinking it."

"Wow. Your head's gonna get even bigger."

"Ha-ha, very funny."

Dan started the car and turned on the radio. "Wristband" by Paul Simon was playing and Red started singing along. He paused his singing just long enough to say, "I love this song. This guy could sing about a dog turd and I would listen. 'Wristband, my man, you've got to have a wristband'—"

"You sing like you're choking on a dog turd," Dan said.

"Yeah. Well … you are a dog turd."

"Good comeback."

Chapter Six

"I'm sorry. What more can I say?" Dan asked. He sat in his recliner staring at the TV and trying his hardest not to make eye contact with Maxine. He had picked Maxine up at work thirty minutes earlier and the ride home was dead silence. Dan knew he would be in trouble when they reached their destination, so he drove along as slowly as he could. They had been arguing now for what seemed to Dan like an eternity.

"Look at me when I'm talking to you!" Maxine shouted.

Visions of Foghorn Leghorn hollering, "Look at me when I'm talkin' to ya, boy!" danced through Dan's mind and he did his best not to grin. It's hard to keep a straight face when you possess the mind of a child. He turned his head in the direction of the shouting. "They're giving me an award, for chrissakes," he offered.

"Key West has a city's biggest idiot award?" Maxine asked.

"Ouch."

"How many times have I asked you not to keep things like this from me?"

Dan screwed up his face in mock concentration. "Seven?"

"One of the paramedics told me you were so drunk you threw up in the street."

"I wasn't drunk, I had a hangover. Big difference."

Maxine doubled her fists. "I could scream."

"I thought you had been."

"What is wrong with you? You're not normal."

"I am normal. My mother had me tested," Dan grinned.

"Is everything a joke to you?"

Dan's eyes shot to the bar on the other side of the dining room. A half-empty bottle of tequila was shouting his name. "You know, when you yell at me like this it makes me want to drink."

"Bullshit! Being a moron makes you want to drink. How much have you drunk today?"

"I haven't had a drop to drink in twenty-nine hours and thirty-seven minutes."

"That's great! I'm going to bed." Maxine spun around and headed toward the hallway. "And that recliner is going to the Goodwill. It looks like shit next to the new furniture."

Where did that come from, Dan thought. "When you talk about getting rid of my recliner," he shouted back, "it makes me want to drink!"

"Screw you!"

"Is that an offer?"

Maxine's reply was the slamming of the bedroom door.

"I guess not."

Chapter Seven

Thursday morning started almost the same way as Wednesday morning. Dan's cell phone vibrated on the nightstand, awakening him at six-twenty. He climbed quietly out of bed and went to his dresser for a pair of running shorts and a T-shirt. He sat down at the end of the bed, slipped his feet into his sneakers, and tied them. He glanced over his shoulder; there was enough light in the room for him to see that Maxine's eyes were closed. He knew she was awake; she was the type who would wake up at the sound of a flea's fart.

Must still be mad, Dan thought. *She probably won't have any breakfast waiting for me when I get back from my run.*

He stood and walked toward the bedroom door. The room started to spin and his stomach turned. He grabbed the edge of the dresser for support. *Holy shit. I don't feel so good.*

The room slowed, and he walked down the hall to the bathroom. Shutting the door behind him he stood in front of the toilet wondering if he was going to throw up. A chill ran up his back and down his arms; he shivered. He side-stepped to the sink and turned on the cold water. After splashing a couple handfuls on his face he felt a little better.

Dan dried his face on the towel that hung over the shower curtain rod, turned back toward the toilet and took a leak, and left the room after remembering to put the seat down.

As he walked past Buddy, who was lying on his bed, he said, "Morning, pal," and went out the door.

When he got to the end of the pathway that led from the sidewalk to the front steps he stretched his arms over his head and groaned. His back and neck seemed to ache more than usual, so did his knees. He had a headache and he was still a little nauseous. He tried to talk himself out of running. *Maybe I shouldn't run two days in a row*, he thought. He looked over his shoulder at the front door and thought about going back inside. Then he looked across the street and saw Edna McGee staring at him through her front window. He waved and she waved back. He turned right and took off running.

*****

Dan finished his run at the corner of Grove Street and Beach View Street and walked the last half a block to his house. When he walked through the front door he could smell the sausage. Maxine was making breakfast. The smell reminded him of his nausea.

"I don't feel very good," he said, as he entered the kitchen.

"Where don't you feel good?" Maxine asked.

"First in the bedroom, then outside, and now here in the kitchen," Dan replied.

Maxine slowly turned around. "I mean, where on your body?"

"My head hurts and I have an upset stomach."

Maxine approached him and put her palm on his forehead. "You don't have a fever."

"I'm achy too."

"You feel like eating?"

"No."

"Why don't you go get in the shower and I'll just fix you some dry toast." Maxine leaned in for a kiss.

Dan pulled back. "I don't want to give you what I have."

Maxine turned back toward the stove. "I don't think I can catch what's happening to you."

"What's that supposed to mean?"

"Just go get in the shower."

******

After his shower, Dan put on a pair of pajama bottoms, a long-sleeved T-shirt, socks, house slippers, and his robe.

"Warm enough?" Maxine asked, when he returned to the kitchen.

"I'm having chills. I think I'm getting the flu," Dan replied.

"Yeah, the flu," Maxine repeated. "Go sit down and I'll put in that toast.

"I'm gonna go sit out back. Can you bring it out to me?"

"Sure."

"And some orange juice? I think I need the vitamin C."

"Yeah, you probably do."

Dan started out the back door and then looked back. "Where's the dog?" he asked.

"I let him out. He probably ran over to Bev's."

"Yeah, probably," Dan responded. He walked down the steps, and down the gravel pathway that led to the two Adirondack chairs that sat next to the fire pit. He sat down in one of the chairs and stared at his dog that lay on his neighbor's deck.

"Come here, boy!" Dan shouted.

Buddy raised his head, saw it was Dan, and dropped his head back to the deck.

"Bastard." Dan crossed his legs, folded his arms across his chest, and waited for his toast.

Bev's back door swung open and she walked out onto the deck. She bent over and scratched Buddy's head. Dan could see she was talking to the dog, but he couldn't hear what she was saying.

Bev straightened up, looked over at Dan, and smiled. "Read about you in the paper this morning," she called out.

"Yeah," Dan hollered back.

Bev leaned against the railing. "Said they're giving you a citation."

"Yeah."

"You don't sound too excited."

"I think I'm coming down with something."

"I'll stay over here then."

"Probably a good idea."

"What's your nurse say about it?"

"She's not too concerned."

Just then Dan's back door opened and Maxine walked out carrying a plate of toast in one hand, a glass of orange juice in the other, and the morning edition of the Key West Citizen folded under her arm. "Here ya go," she said.

"Thanks."

"How ya feeling?"

"A little better. I hope it doesn't last long, Me and Red are supposed to get our plaques on Tuesday."

"It'll be gone by then … one way or another."

"What do ya mean? What do you think it is?"

"Withdrawals."

"Withdrawals? Withdrawals from what?" Dan asked defensively.

Maxine cocked her head but said nothing.

"I don't drink enough to have withdrawals," said Dan.

"Obviously you do," Maxine argued.

"But I don't drink *that* much."

"Dan, your body is detoxing. It may not be as bad as a severe alcoholic detox, but you're going to feel some discomfort for a few days."

"*Some* discomfort. I feel terrible."

"Well, that's just because you're a man and everything feels worse to a man."

"What's that supposed to mean?"

"You're all big babies."

Dan sighed heavily. "I just can't believe this."

"Believe it. When was the last time you stopped drinking?"

"I've never stopped drinking."

"That's why you've never felt like this before."

"I need a drink."

"Yes, you do, but that doesn't mean you have to have one. Just take it one day at a time."

"I don't want to stop forever. I just want to slow down."

"Okay."

"I'll just stop for a while … just to let my body rest."

"Sounds like a good idea."

"A few days, you say."

"Yes."

"I can do this for a few days."

"I know you can."

"This sucks."

Buddy jumped up and ran from Bev's deck and lay down beside Dan's chair. He put his chin on Dan's foot. Dan reached down and petted the dog's head. "Thanks, pal. I needed that."

Chapter Eight

By Saturday morning Dan was feeling a little better and Maxine had the day off from work. Dan lay in his hammock smoking a Don Mateo cigar and staring up through the palm fronds at the clouds that floated above him. Buddy lay on his belly under the hammock. It was seventy-eight degrees with a slight breeze blowing off the water.

Maxine sat in one of the Adirondack chairs reading the morning paper and drinking a cup of coffee.

Dan inhaled and then loudly exhaled.

Maxine glanced over. "What's the matter, baby?" she asked.

"I'm bored," Dan replied.

"Why don't you go see Red?" Maxine suggested.

"I don't want to hang around the bar."

"Why don't you go see one of your other friends?"

"Like who?"

"Oh yeah, sorry. I forgot. You don't have any other friends."

"Ouch."

"You could run over to the center and see Mel."

"Christ, Maxine, I'm trying *not* to drink."

"How about Phil? You haven't been over to Phil and April's in a while. Why don't you see if he wants to go fishing or something?"

Dan shrugged. "Phil's always busy. It's hard to be friends with people who have real jobs."

"Then I don't know what to tell you." Maxine flipped through the pages and read the headlines stopping every once in a while on stories that sounded interesting to her. "Don't you have anything to work on?"

"Like what?"

"You haven't played private detective in almost a week."

"*Played* private detective? You hate when I play private detective."

"I hate when you lay around in your hammock smoking cigars and complaining about being bored."

"Sorry. Nobody's called lately."

"Give Rick a call, maybe he has something for you to do."

"Like what, mop the floors at the police station?" Dan asked sarcastically.

"You're probably not qualified for that," Maxine responded. "I meant go over there and see if there's something he needs help on. A case they can't solve or something."

Dan shot her a condescending look. "It doesn't work like that, Maxine. It's not like in the movies or on TV."

"Sorry. Just trying to help."

"Yeah, I know." Dan dropped his head and took a long drag on the cigar. Something near the house caught his eye; he turned his head to look. It was a red rubber ball about the same size as a bowling ball, and it was bouncing down the gravel path that went from the driveway to the backyard.

Dan watched as the ball bounced toward him and Maxine. Maxine caught its movement and looked up from her paper. They looked at each other and back at the ball. Seconds later a young boy about nine years old rounded the corner of the house, running after the ball; he stopped it with his foot just before it hit the fire pit.

The youngster had red hair and light skin with freckles covering his nose and cheeks. He wore cut-off jeans, sneakers and a blue T-shirt.

"Hi," the boy said.

"Hi," Maxine replied.

Dan said nothing.

Buddy jumped to his feet and stared at the boy. He let out a quiet bark.

"Does your dog bite?" the boy asked.

"He's not my dog," Dan responded.

"Whose is he?"

"Nobody's. He just lives here."

"That's weird."

"Maybe you're weird."

"What's his name?"

"Buddy," said Maxine. "And he doesn't bite. What's your name?"

"Orrin."

"Orrin what?"

"Orrin Maxwell Stein."

"Where are you from, Orrin Maxwell Stein?" Maxine asked.

Orrin bent to pick up the ball. "Maine."

"What are you doing in Florida?"

"Visiting my grandmother."

"What are you doing in my backyard?" Dan asked.

"Getting my ball. We're playing kickball in the street." Orrin slapped his thigh. "Come here, boy."

Buddy ran to Orrin and pushed his head against the boy's leg.

"Who's your grandmother?" Dan asked.

Orrin was absorbed in petting Buddy. Maxine looked at Dan and said, "The Steins live across the street next door to Edna McGee. You'd know if you weren't so antisocial."

"Oh."

"What are ya doin'?" another boy called out as he made his way down the path.

"Playin' with these guys's dog!" Orrin shouted back.

"Oh great, they're multiplying," Dan mumbled.

The second boy had brown hair and dark skin. He wore cargo shorts and a plaid short-sleeved button-up shirt.

"And what's your name?" Maxine asked.

"Julian Thompson," the boy replied.

"Carl and Emma Thompson's boy?" Maxine asked.

"Uh-huh," Julian answered.

"Who the hell is Carl and Emma Thompson?' Dan asked.

Maxine shook her head. "They live two houses down," Maxine replied, pointing in the opposite direction of Bev's house.

"Oh," said Dan.

Julian began petting Buddy as well.

"Well, ya got your ball," Dan said. "You might as well move along."

Julian looked from Dan to Maxine. "Your dad's grumpy," he said.

Maxine cackled in delight. "He's not my dad," she responded.

"And that's why I hate kids," said Dan.

"Does he just live with you?" Orrin asked Maxine.

"No!" Dan shouted. "*She* lives with *me*."

"Why?" Orrin asked.

"Because I'm rich," Dan replied.

"Oh," said Orrin. "You look a lot older than her. And you don't look rich."

"Well, I'm not *a lot* older than her." Dan took a drag on his stogie.

"How come you smoke cigars?" Julian asked. "My mom said smoking is gross and bad for you."

"Oh yeah? Well, your mom's wrong," Dan responded. "Smoking makes you look cool." Dan wrapped his index and middle fingers around the cigar and puffed away, blowing smoke rings into the air. "See that? Looks cool. And cool people have more friends."

"Dan!" Maxine scolded. "You can't say that to kids. He's just joking, guys. Smoking *is* gross, and it is bad for you."

"Whatever," said Dan. "Maybe his mother should teach him not to question grown-ups."

"I bet you can't even run fast because you smoke," Orrin said.

"I bet I can," Dan replied.

"Can not."

"Can too."

"Can not."

"Can too."

"Prove it," Julian said.

"I don't have to prove anything to you," said Dan.

"Wow," Maxine groaned. "It's like I have a child of my own."

"I bet we can beat you at kick ball," Orrin said.

"Bet you can't," Dan said.

"He'll probably die of a heart attack," Julian pointed out.

"*You'll* probably die of a boot in your ass," said Dan as he climbed out of the hammock.

"What are you doing?" Maxine asked.

"I'm gonna kick some ass at kick ball," Dan replied.

"Oh, brother," said Maxine. "Don't hurt him boys."

"We won't," Orrin said.

Dan slapped the ball out of the boy's hand and got right in his face. "That's right you won't, 'cause you're going down, ladies!"

Chapter Nine

Dan entered the street dribbling the ball. Two other boys and a girl stood at the edge of the street, in Edna's yard.

Julian pointed to the others one at a time. "That's Tommy, that's Allen, and that's Sarah."

"You guys playing too?" Dan asked.

The three kids nodded their heads yes.

"What are the teams?" Julian asked.

"I'll take the girl," Dan answered. "She looks tougher than the rest of you."

Sarah smiled, and walked into the street.

"You two against the four of us?" Tommy asked.

"That's right," Dan replied. "We kick first."

Tommy pointed out the bases as he took the field.

Dan turned to Sarah. "I'll kick first, then you can bring me home," he said with a wink.

"Okay," said Sarah.

Dan tossed the ball to Julian and readied himself.

Julian glanced over his shoulders one at a time at his teammates, making sure they were where they were supposed to be. He rolled the ball as hard as he could at home plate, which was a manhole cover. The "pitching mound" was a bump in the asphalt.

Dan took a step back and then kicked as hard as he could … missing the ball completely. The opposing team erupted in laughter.

"That was just a practice kick!" Dan shouted. "Just a practice kick."

Sarah bent over and scooped the ball into her arms and threw it back to Julian. "Good try," she whispered. "You'll get it next time."

"Thanks, Sarah," said Dan.

"Car!" one of the outfielders shouted, and the kids scattered to the curb.

Dan, rubbing his leg, looked up to see Skip Stoner's yellow Volkswagen Thing coming down the street, with Red Baxter sitting in the passenger seat.

Skip pulled to the curb and shut off the engine.

"You can't park there," Dan informed him. "We're playing a game here, for chrissakes!"

"Ooh, sorry, dude," Skip replied in his Jeff surfer-esque way of speaking. "I'll pull forward a bit."

Skip moved the car down the street another fifty yards and the two men climbed from the vehicle.

"What are you guys doing here?" Dan asked.

"We came to check on ya," Red answered. "Make sure you were okay."

"Why wouldn't I be?"

"Red Man said you were on the wagon, bro," said Skip. "We thought we'd come over and show our support."

"Gee, thanks," Dan said.

"Are we gonna play, or what?" Allen asked.

"Red, you're with me," Dan said. "Skip, you're with those guys."

"Alright!" Skip hollered. "Let's do this, little dudes." He held out his hands for the ball.

"What?" Julian asked.

"Throw me the ball, bro. I'm gonna pitch."

"I'm pitching … *bro*." Julian pointed up the street. "*You're* in the outfield."

"Ha! Shot down," said Red.

"Whatever, dudes," Skip lumbered up the street to his position. "That's bogus."

Julian rolled the ball once again and Dan kicked it over Skip's head. Skip turned and took off running like a bat out of hell, and Dan did the same in the direction of first base—Edna's mailbox. All the children were shouting orders at Skip.

Dan reached second base—a big oil stain in the street—just as Skip grabbed the ball. Skip threw the ball as hard as he could.

Tommy positioned himself at third base, fire hydrant.

Dan and the ball reached third at the exact time.

"Safe!" Red and Sarah shouted in unison.

"Out!" the other boys hollered.

Maxine, who had walked around the house and was now sitting on the front steps, yelled, "Tie goes to the runner!"

Everyone's head turned in her direction.

"What?" Maxine asked. "I've played kickball before. I know the rules."

"You heard her," Dan grinned. "Tie goes to the runner."

Sarah was up next. She made it to first, sending Dan to home. Then Red kicked a home run making it three to zero.

The game ended after about forty-five minutes when two of the boys were called in for dinner. Soon after a few more went home and only Skip, Dan, Red, and Sarah were left standing in the street.

The four walked to the steps where Maxine sat with a glass of Mascato; she high-fived them all. "Good game," she congratulated them.

"Yeah, but I thought we had 'em," Dan replied. He was panting hard from the exertion and sweating buckets. *Maybe I sweated off some of the excess booze in my system*, he thought sardonically.

"My guys were just too darn good, bro," said Skip. "But you guys put up a valiant effort."

"Thanks, Skip," Sarah said. She sat down on the steps below Maxine, placed her elbows on her knees, and rested her chin in her hands.

Maxine smiled at the little girl. "Do you have to be home for dinner, Sarah?" she asked.

"Nope," replied Sarah.

"Did you already eat supper?"

"Nope."

"Did you have lunch?"

"Yup. I ate lunch at the Thompsons'."

"What's your last name?" Skip asked.

"Tinka."

Skip cocked his head. "Is your mom Anna?"

"Yeah, do you know her?"

"Um, yeah … kinda."

"What street do you live on?" Dan asked. "I've never seen you around here before."

"I play over here almost every day. I live on Sky View Street, right behind Mrs. McGee."

Buddy crawled over to the bottom step and placed his chin on the tread. Sarah leaned over and scratched him between his ears. "Buddy knows me," she remarked.

Red stretched his arms over his head and let out a little groan. "Well, I guess I better be getting back to the bar," he said. "You gonna be in later?"

"I don't think so," Dan replied. "I think I'll just hang around the house tonight."

Red slapped his pal on the back. "Maybe I'll see you tomorrow then. Good game. Come on Skip, let's hit the road."

Skip said, "Check ya later, Dan the man." The two men turned, and walked up the street to Skip's car.

"What do you want for dinner?" Maxine asked.

"I dunno. Pizza?" Dan replied.

Maxine placed her hand on top of Sarah's head. "Would you like to stay for dinner, Sarah?"

Dan quickly shook his head no.

58

"Sure, thanks, Maxine."

Dan rolled his eyes and walked up the steps past them. "I'm gonna take a shower."

Maxine raised her empty wine glass. "Refill first?"

"Sure," Dan said.

"You want something to drink, Sarah? A soda, or something," Maxine asked.

"Water's fine. Thanks."

"Comin' right up," Dan sighed.

Chapter Ten

Dan sat in his recliner with a glass of 7UP on the end table next to him. Maxine and Sarah sat at opposite ends of the couch with their plates balanced on their laps. The television was tuned to MeTV and Dan's eyes were glue to an old episode of *The Incredible Hulk*. Dan had never been able to figure out why David Banner's shirt got ripped to shreds whenever he turned into the Hulk, yet his pants stayed pretty much intact. One of the wonders of science, he supposed.

"Does your mom work every night, Sarah?" Maxine asked.

Sarah swallowed her bite of pizza before she spoke. "Most nights. Some days, too."

"What does she do?"

"She's a secretary."

Dan glanced over at Maxine with one eyebrow raised and then back at the TV.

"Where is she a secretary?" Maxine inquired.

Sarah shrugged. "For some lawyer," she replied. "Can I use your bathroom, please?"

"Sure. It's right down the hall on the right."

Sarah placed her plate on the couch cushion and walked to the bathroom.

When Dan heard the door shut and lock he turned to Maxine. "A secretary who works on Saturday nights?"

"I'm sure there are secretaries who work on the weekends, Dan," Maxine said. "What do you think, she's lying to us?"

"I didn't say she was lying to us … maybe her mother is lying to *her*."

"Oh, come on, you're always so suspicious of everyone."

"I can't help being suspicious. It's part of my job."

"You don't have a job." Maxine took a bite of her pizza.

"You know what I mean."

They heard the bathroom door open and ended their conversation. Buddy raised his head from his bed and watched Sarah cross the room. She took a seat back on the couch and watched the Hulk kicking ass and taking names as she finished her pizza.

"Are you supposed to be home by a certain time?" Maxine asked.

"I have to be in the house at eight o'clock," Sarah responded.

"It's almost eight. Would you like Dan to walk you home?"

Dan went limp and rolled his eyes.

"No, that's okay. I can walk home by myself," Sarah said.

"I know you can, but I would feel better if Dan walked you home."

"She said she can do it on her own," Dan argued.

Sarah thought about it for a second and said, "Sure, he can walk me home if you want him to."

"Thank you," said Maxine.

"Come on," Dan said as he climbed out of his La-Z-Boy. "Let's go. It's almost time for *Wonder Woman*."

"And we wouldn't want to miss that," Maxine added.

"Damn—I mean, dang right we wouldn't," Dan said. He also wondered if the same thing that held Banner's pants together, kept Wonder Woman's boobs on the inside of that skimpy costume.

"Thank you for the pizza, Maxine" Sarah said.

"I paid for it," Dan pointed out.

"You're welcome," Maxine said. "Come back anytime."

Dan's eyes widened and he shook his head. "Yeah, come back anytime," he grumbled. "I love having kids around. Maybe I'll even get a few of my own." As they walked past Buddy, Dan said, "Come on, dog, you can walk over with us, too."

"Shouldn't you put a leash on him?" Sarah asked. She grinned impishly and added: "I mean Buddy, not Mr. Dan."

"Hardy-har-har," Dan replied. "Maybe we should put one on *you*?"

"Dan," Maxine scolded, and the three walked out the door.

They crossed the street and walked down the side of Edna McGee's house, through her backyard, and out onto Sky View Street. Dan felt Edna's eyes on him the whole time. He was used to it; she was the personification of the "neighborhood watch."

"Which house is yours?" Dan asked.

Sarah pointed at a one story ranch with wooden clapboards and shutters. A red and black MINI Cooper sat in the driveway. "That one right there," she said with a smile "My mom's home already. She doesn't usually get home this early."

Dan and Sarah walked across the street and down two houses; Buddy followed close behind.

When they got to the concrete walkway that lead from the sidewalk to the house, Sarah said, "Thank you for walking me home, Mr. Dan."

Dan stopped on the sidewalk. "I'll wait here until you get in the house."

When Sarah was halfway to the house the front porch light came on and a woman opened the door.

"Hi, Mom," Sarah said.

Her mother stepped out onto the porch. "Who's that?" she asked.

Dan stepped toward the house and into the light. "I'm Dan Coast. I live over on Beach View."

"He's my friend, Mom," Sarah offered.

"Come in the house, honey," said her mother.

"See ya, Mr. Dan," Sarah called out as she walked into the house. "Thanks for the pizza."

"You must be Anna," Dan said.

Anna stepped further out onto the porch and shut the door behind her. "What are you doing with my daughter? What are you, some kind of weirdo?"

Dan smiled nervously. "No, ma'am. See, what happened is, Sarah said she hadn't eaten dinner so we—me and my girlfriend—invited her in for pizza."

"Just stay away from her from now on. You hear me?"

"Yeah … whatever. Nice to meet you too." Dan turned and started back across the street. "Come on, dog."

When Dan walked back inside his own house Maxine was still seated on the couch. "How'd it go?" she asked.

Dan plopped down in his recliner. "Thanks for that," he said.

"Thanks for what."

"Her mother called me a weirdo for hanging out with little girls."

Maxine chuckled.

"Yeah, real funny. I'll probably end up on some list now because of you."

"Because of me?"

"Yeah. You're the one who invited her in here and fed her. Kids are like cats and dogs; they keep coming back if you feed them. And you're the one who made me walk her home. From now on I'll probably be known around here as that weirdo who follows little girls home after dark."

"Well, she said she hadn't had supper. I was just trying too—"

"Shh," Dan said with a finger to his lips as the theme music started to play. "Wonder Woman's on."

Chapter Eleven

Sunday morning after breakfast Dan stood at the front door looking out through the glass at the street.

Maxine walked in from the kitchen. "What's the matter, none of your friends out front playing?"

"Funny," said Dan.

"Why don't you go knock on Tommy's door and see if he can come out and play?"

"Enough." Dan reached into his pocket, pulled out his cell phone, and dialed. "Hey what's up?" he asked.

"Just having breakfast," Rick Carver replied. "What's up with you?"

"I'm bored."

"Okay. Is there something I can do about that?"

Dan looked over his shoulder at Maxine, who was clearing the breakfast dishes from the dining room table. "Hold on," he said, stepping out onto the porch and pulled the door shut behind him. "I was just wondering if you had anything for me to do."

"What do you mean?"

Dan hesitated. "Like … down at the police station."

"You mean like mopping the floors?"

"No, Rick, not like mopping the floors."

"What exactly are you asking me, Coast?"

"Like … do you have any cases I could help with?"

"Hell yeah! As a matter of fact, I was hoping you would call."

Dan smiled. "Really?"

"No, you asshole, not really. What do you mean, a case you could help with? Do I need to remind you that you're not a cop? You're not even a private cop. You have no license."

"Well, you don't have to be so mean about it. I just thought that because we're friends and all you'd throw me a bone. I saw in a movie once where this guy would solved cold cases in his spare time."

"Really, Dan? You saw it in a movie once and you thought it looked like fun? Police work is serious business. It's not for amateurs."

This coming from the Goodyear blimp version of Barney Fife, Dan mused. "Come on, Rick, there must be something I can do. I'm bored as shit and I'm going out of my mind."

"Sounds like you've already gone out of your mind. Why don't you do what you usually do—go hang out at Red's and get drunk every day?"

"That's cold, Rick," said Dan. "I'm trying not to drink.

"Whoa, wait ... what?" Rick tapped several times on his cell phone. "I think my phones broken, because it sounded like you said you were trying not to drink."

"Seriously, Rick, I haven't had a drink in quite a while."

"By quite a while, do you mean an hour and a half?"

"More like five days."

"Seriously? You're not pulling my nut sack?"

"Not if you paid me. No, really, and it's a lot tougher than I thought. I have nothing to do, and that makes it even harder."

Rick sighed loudly. "I'll see what I can do ... but I'm not promising you anything."

"Thanks, Rick."

"Yeah. Just don't make me regret it." Rick hung up the phone and Dan stepped back inside.

"Who were you talking to?" Maxine asked.

"Rick."

Maxine grinned. "Took my advice, did ya?"

"Quiet, woman."

Maxine did her best Dan Coast impersonation. "Don't be ridiculous, Maxine. It's not like it is in the movies, Maxine," she gloated.

"Shut it."

Maxine swatted his ass affectionately. "Don't you know that imitation is the sincerest form of flattery?"

"Tell that to Rich Little."

"Who?"

"Never mind." Dan walked toward the kitchen. "Come on, dog," he commanded as he passed Buddy's bed. "Let's walk out to the beach."

Buddy leaped to his feet and followed his pal through the house and out the back door. Together they walked down the gravel path past the fire pit and the hammock. Along the way Dan stooped to grab Buddy's tennis ball. When Dan reached the beach he tossed the ball into the water. Buddy dropped to his belly in the sand. "Really?" Dan asked. "I'm not going out there and getting that ball." Buddy ignored him.

A Frisbee ricocheted off the trunk of a palm tree and landed three feet to Dan's right. He looked over to see Julian Thompson running his way, and close behind was Orrin Stein.

Julian bent to pick up the Frisbee. "Hey, Dan," he said.

"Hey, Julian," Dan replied.

"Hi, Dan," Orrin called out. "Hey, Buddy."

"Hey, Orrin," said Dan. He rubbed his eyes with his palms. *What the Christ*, he thought. *Almost four years of purposely avoiding the neighbors and now I'm on a first-name basis with their friggin kids.*

"Can Buddy catch a Frisbee?" Julian inquired.

"I don't know," Dan replied. "You'd have to ask him."

"Can you catch a Frisbee, Buddy?" Julian asked.

"I just threw his ball out in the water and he has no interest in getting that," said Dan.

"Go get your ball," Orrin commanded.

Buddy jumped up and ran splashing into the water after the tennis ball.

"Great," said Dan, shaking his head.

When Buddy returned with the ball he dropped it at Orrin's bare feet.

Julian threw the Frisbee down the beach as hard as he could. "Get the Frisbee!" he shouted, and Buddy took off running.

"Smart dog," Orrin commented.

"Yeah, he's a friggin genius," Dan responded. "You should see him lick his own ass. A regular Einstein."

Orrin and Julian snickered. "Lick his own butt," Julian said. Dan had to grin at the little boy's self-censorship.

Buddy ran back to the group with the Frisbee. Orrin took it from his mouth.

"You want to play Frisbee?" Julian asked.

Dan glanced back over his shoulder at the house. "I'll tell you what," he said. "One of you guys run up to my house and knock on the back door and tell Maxine to grab me a cigar. Fetch it back and I'll play catch with ya."

"You want one of us to bring you the cigar?" Julian asked hesitantly.

"Yeah, why?" Dan asked. "Is that too far for ya to walk?"

"I don't think I'm supposed to hold cigars or cigarettes," the young boy answered.

"Why not?" Dan asked. "They don't bite."

"My dad would be mad."

"Because you carried a cigar? Why?"

"My dad says they're bad for ya. People get cancer and stuff."

Orrin looked on quietly.

"Does he think you're gonna get finger cancer from carrying a cigar?" Dan asked.

Julian shrugged.

"Well, ya can't," Dan said.

"I'll get it for ya," said Orrin eagerly. He handed the Frisbee to Dan and took off running toward the house.

"Sorry," said Julian.

Dan stepped back and tossed him the Frisbee. "Don't worry about it, pal. It ain't your fault … it's your dad's."

Julian grinned and threw the Frisbee back to Dan.

"Hey, uh, you know where Sarah's mom works? Dan asked.

Julian got a strange look on his face. He turned his head in every direction, searching the immediate area for eavesdroppers, and leaned in as though he was giving Dan the secret launch codes. Dan did the same in an overly-animated fashion.

"She works for the phone company," Julian whispered.

Dan's eyes widened. "The phone company?"

Julian nodded. "But don't say I said anything."

"Your secret is safe with me."

Dan pointed down the beach and Julian ran backwards in that direction. When he was far enough away Dan hurled the plastic disc. Buddy ran down the beach as well, his eyes fixed on the Frisbee. Julian snagged it out of the air.

"Good catch!" Dan shouted.

Julian grinned proudly and threw it back. Buddy gave chase again. Dan caught the Frisbee behind his back.

"Awesome!" Julian shouted.

Dan looked to his right to see Orrin returning with the cigar, cutter, and lighter. "Here ya go, Dan," said the boy.

"Thanks, pal," said Dan.

Orrin turned and ran to join his friend.

Dan threw the Frisbee once again. While the boys chased it he snipped the tip of his cigar, lit it, and took a big drag. The three continued to play catch for another half hour or so, with Buddy running back and forth like he was the key player in an intense game of Keep Away.

Dan's cell phone vibrated in his pocket, he reached for it and answered. "Hello?"

"It's Rick."

"I know."

"Stop down to the station tomorrow morning around ten. I think I might have something for ya."

"Awesome! Thanks, Rick."

"Like I said, don't make me regret this. And not a word about it to anyone."

"You got it, Rick." Dan hung up the phone and dropped it back into his pocket just as the Frisbee hit him in the forehead. "Goddammit!" he shouted.

Both boys had looks of horror on their faces.

"Sorry," Julian called out.

"Ya gotta wait till I'm looking!" Dan shouted back. He rubbed his forehead with the tips of his fingers. "Shit, that hurt like a bitch!"

Dan noticed Julian and Orrin heading down the beach away from him.

"Hey, where you guys going?" he shouted.

"Home," said Julian.

"How come? We were just starting to have fun."

"You swear too much," Julian replied. Orrin bobbed his head in agreement.

Dan hung his head in something close to shame.

Chapter Twelve

At eight o'clock Monday morning Dan pulled his Porsche to the curb on Thompson Street in front of Red's house, and gave the horn a short toot. A few seconds later Red's front door opened and out he came. The big bow-legged man rocked back and forth as he walked. He was wearing an old, ratty, red T-shirt tucked tightly into his olive green cargo shorts. On the front of the shirt was a picture of the Kool-Aid Man.

"Oh yeah!" exclaimed Red, doing a pretty fair impression of the mascot's catchphrase as he pointed at the logo.

Dan shook his head. "Nice shirt. Laundry day?"

"Found it at the bottom of my drawer. I've had this shirt for years."

"Looks brand new," Dan said, noticing the two small tears and the mustard stain.

Red walked around to the passenger side and climbed in. "My wife used to hate this shirt. Said it was childish."

"I can't believe it." Dan put the car into drive and started down the street.

"I know, right? She can't stop me now."

"Boy, you sure showed her."

"Yup. She got the house, the car, and one of the pizza shops, but I still got the shirt … bitch."

"Where do you want to go for breakfast?"

"You're paying, you decide."

"I don't remember saying I was paying."

"I don't remember you saying you weren't."

"Pepe's?" Dan suggested.

"Nah, we went there last time."

"Banana Cafe?"

"Sounds good."

Dan took a left onto White Street and then a right at Catherine Street.

"So, why do we have to be to the police station at ten?" Red asked.

"Rick wants to talk to me about something."

"Probably about getting our citations tomorrow. What are you wearing?"

"What am I wearing?"

"Are you dressing up?"

"Hadn't really thought about it."

"We should dress up, right?"

"I don't know. I guess. I'll see what Maxine says."

"Well, make sure you let me know."

"Don't worry, pal, I'll let you know what I'm wearing. I wouldn't want us to show up in the same dress."

Dan took a left onto Duval and began searching for a parking spot.

"Oh, by the way," Red said. "You know that little girl that was playing kickball the other day? What was her name?"

"Sarah?"

"Yeah, her. Guess what her mom does for a living."

"I know what she does for a living," said Dan. "She works for the phone company."

"Um, no, she's a call girl."

"Who told you that?"

"Skip. He dated a friend of hers once."

"Huh."

"Who told you she worked for the phone company."

"Julian."

"Who the hell is Julian?"

"One of the neighborhood kids. We were playing Frisbee yesterday and—"

"Whoa, wait. You were playing Frisbee? You're not gonna start going to sleep-overs and shit, are ya?"

"Shut up, dickhead. The kids asked me if I wanted to play, so I played."

"It's your story, pal."

Dan whipped into a spot. "Anyway, I asked him what her mother did and he said she worked for the phone company, but he was all hush-hush about it, and told me not to tell anyone."

"Huh. Weird."

The two men climbed from the vehicle and started walking the two blocks back to the Banana Cafe. Up ahead of them, Red recognized someone standing at the corner. "Hey, there's that guy from the other day," he said.

"What guy?"

"That homeless guy."

As they neared, the man looked at them and smiled. Red smiled back.

"Sure is," Dan agreed.

"Look, he's got a brand new pair of pants, and a new backpack," Red pointed out proudly. "I helped pay for that."

"Ya did, did ya?"

"Well, I gave him five bucks."

"I wonder where he was able to find a five-dollar pair of pants." Dan asked.

"Very funny. I think I'll give him another five bucks."

"Heart o' gold," said Dan.

"How ya doin', pal?" Red asked.

"Good," the old man replied. Despite his grizzled appearance, he held himself with dignity, and intelligence sparkled in his deep-set eyes.

Red held out the fiver and the old man reached out his wrinkled, bony hand.

"Here ya go, pal," Red said.

"Bless you," said the old man.

Red smiled and glanced over at Dan.

The old man turned to Dan. "How ya doin', Dan?" he asked.

Red's smile started to fade.

"Good, Mr. Dutcher," Dan replied.

Red looked confused.

Dutcher looked down at his new jeans. "Thanks for the pants, Dan, and the backpack," he said, humbly.

"Don't mention it," Dan replied. "Did you call that guy?"

"Yes, thanks. I have a meeting with him tomorrow. He said they're gonna set me up in my own place. Thanks again for everything."

"Hey, what are friends for?" Dan replied.

A cell phones ring tone began playing The Band's "Up Cripple Creek," which startled the old man. "Oh! That's me," he said, and reached into his pocket. "Oh, yeah, and thanks for the phone."

Dan smiled.

"Hello?" said Dutcher. "How can I help you?"

Dan started walking and slapped Dutcher on the back as he passed. "You take care of yourself, Mr. Dutcher.

Dutcher responded with a wink as he listened intently to whoever had called him.

Dan held the door for Red when they reached the Banana Cafe. As Red walked in, Dan couldn't resist commenting, "Every little bit helps."

"Shut up," Red replied angrily. "Just shut up."

Chapter Thirteen

At ten minutes after ten Dan and Red walked into Chief Rick Carver's office. Rick glanced up from his paperwork and peered over the top of his reading glasses, with the usual expression of annoyance. Dan was engaged with his sidekick in one of the inane conversations that rick knew all too well.

"It's milestone, ya moron," Dan chuckled, "not mildstone."

"I think you're wrong," said Red.

"You're late," Rick informed them, and nodded toward Red. "And what's he doing here?"

"He's my helper," Dan replied.

"What can he do?"

"He can hand out five-dollar bills to the needy."

"You're such a dick," Red declared.

"I told you I didn't want to regret this and I already am." Rick tossed three file folders on his desk.

Dan reached for one of the folders.

"Wait!" Rick said, and slapped Dan's hand. "I'm gonna leave the room for a few minutes to get a cup of coffee."

"You want me to wait till you get back to look at these?" Dan asked.

"Are you an idiot?" Rick replied.

"He is," said Red.

"Oh, you want me to look at them while you're gone," Dan surmised.

Rick nodded yes. "I knew you'd get it eventually. I'm practicing something called plausible deniability—I wasn't there, so how could I know if you looked at these case files or not. In other words, I'm covering my ass. Ya get it?"

"How very covert," Red pointed out. "Can we take them with us?"

"No you can't take them with you," Rick replied.

Dan pulled his cell from his pocket. "Can I take pictures?"

"No, you can't take pictures. Wow!" Rick was already having second and maybe even third thoughts. "Maybe this was a bad idea."

"No, no," Dan said, dropping the phone back into his pocket. "We'll just look at 'em."

Rick grabbed his coffee mug off of his desk and walked out the door shaking his head. As soon as the door shut behind him, Dan retrieved his phone.

"What are ya doing?" Red asked.

"Taking pictures. What do you think?" Dan responded as he opened the first folder. "Ooh, a murder case from 2010."

Red opened one of the other folders. "A missing person from 2007."

"*Bor*-ing," said Dan as he snapped pictures of each page.

Red closed the folder and opened the last one. "Another murder from 2006."

Dan stopped what he was doing. "Who got killed?"

"Some old guy."

"This one is a thirty-two-year-old woman," said Dan. "Her husband was fifty-one. A May-December deal. Sounds kinda juicy."

"Yeah, let's go with that one," Red agreed.

Dan took pictures of the last two pages and shut the folder just as Rick walked back into the room with his cup of coffee. He walked around his desk and sat in his chair. "Remember, not a word about this to anyone."

"You got it," said Dan. "Oh, and, Rick, one other thing."

"What now?"

"Do you know a woman by the name of Anna Tinka? Lives over on Sky View Street."

"Yeah, I know *of* her," said Rick. "I know she's been arrested a couple times for prostitution. She's one of Papi Garcia's girls. Why do you ask?"

"She's got a little girl."

"Yeah, the kid's been removed from the home at least twice by Child Protective Services. Tinka's got a sister up in Key Largo that takes the kid each time."

"How does she get her back?"

"I'm not sure. But I do know she's never been removed because of abuse."

"That's good to know," said Dan. "She thinks her mom is a secretary,"

"Better than knowing she's a call girl," Rick observed

Dan grinned and looked at Red. "Call girl," he repeated with a knowing nod.

"I don't get it," Rick said.

"A neighborhood kid told me she worked for the phone company."

Red chuckled. "Now I get it. Probably overheard his parents talking about her being a call girl,"

"Now if that's all, get out of my office," Rick said. "And don't be late tomorrow."

Red looked confused.

"What's tomorrow?" Dan asked.

"The citation ceremony!" Rick shouted.

"Oh, yeah, that," said Dan.

"Don't worry, Rick," Red said. "We'll be plenty early."

"You better be."

"What time is the ceremony?" Dan asked.

"Noon," said Rick.

"Will there be an open bar?" Red asked.

"No," Rick replied. "Don't be stupid."

"A buffet?" Red asked.

Rick just glared at him.

"Those little triangle sandwiches?"

"Get out," said Rick.

As the two were about to leave the room, Red paused and turned around. "Will the mayor also be giving us the key to the city, or is it just the plaque."

"It's just a plaque and a citation thanking you for your 'heroism'."

"Hmm, a key to the city would have been nice."

"Please. Leave," Rick ordered calmly.

Dan and Red walked across the parking lot toward Dan's car. "Do you remember anyone ever getting the key to the city?" Red asked.

"Not since I've been here," Dan replied.

Red climbed into the passenger seat. "You think they even *have* a key to the city?"

"It's probably under the doormat at the airport."

"Sure would like to get a key to the city."

"Dream big, my friend. Dream big."

Chapter Fourteen

At six o'clock the following morning Dan's cell phone began vibrating across the top of his nightstand. He let out a groan as he turned over to answer it.

"Hello?"

"Hey, you see the weather report?" Red asked.

"Weather report." Dan's voice cracked and he cleared his throat. "What the Christ are ya talking about? I'm trying to sleep, ya dumb fu—"

"They're saying it might rain this afternoon."

"Big deal."

"Our ceremony is today."

"So what?"

"What if it rains?"

"I'm going back to sleep." Dan hung up the phone.

"Who was that?" Maxine asked.

"The weatherman," Dan replied.

Maxine shrugged and rolled over.

"Hey," said Dan. "Since you're awake."

"I'm not awake."

"You're talking."

"I'm talking in my sleep."

"Can you have sex in your sleep?"

"I usually do."

"Ouch." Dan lifted his leg, and with his big toe hooked into her waistband, began sliding Maxine's pajamas bottoms down to her ankles.

"What are you doing?" she asked.

"I'm not sure. I think my foot is asleep."

Maxine giggled and rolled over to face him. She reached down beneath the covers. "*Something's* wide awake," she said.

"Probably excited about the award ceremony. I'm a hero, ya know."

Maxine pulled off her pajama top in one swift, fluid motion. She pressed her naked body against her boyfriend and kissed him on the lips.

"So I've heard. I don't think I've ever had sex with a hero before."

"Well, Lois Lane, you're in for a friggin' treat."

*****

Dan stood at the back screen door staring up at the sky. He was barefoot and shirtless. He was wearing an old pair of red flannel pajama bottoms that had made the trip south with him years ago. Buddy stood next to Dan with his nose pressed against the screen.

"Pretty cloudy out there," Dan remarked as Maxine walked into the kitchen.

"Is it raining?" she asked.

"Not yet." Dan pushed open the door and Buddy made a run for it. Dan watched as the dog ran around in a circle in the middle of the yard, did his business, and then headed for Bev's.

"I don't know why that dog can't shit over in Bev's yard," Dan wondered aloud.

Maxine walked up behind him, put her arms around him, and rested her head on his back. "He is your dog, Dan."

"True, but he spends just as much time over there."

"We'll bring it up at the next meeting," Maxine joked. "You want me to make you some breakfast?"

Dan turned and kissed her on the forehead. "Why don't you go sit down and I'll make *you* some breakfast?"

"Really?"

"Don't sound so surprised. I've made you breakfast before."

"Seems like it's only after you get sex."

"And what does that tell you?"

"That you're kind of a jerk."

"Exactly. Now, go sit down and relax so I can whip you up something delicious for breakfast."

"Sounds good to me." Maxine spun around and walked back into the living room, turned on the TV, and sat down on the couch. She put her feet up on the coffee table and started surfing through the channels.

"You want strawberry or blueberry Pop-Tarts?" Dan called out.

"Like I said, kind of a jerk," Maxine whispered.

Chapter Fifteen

Guest of honor Dan Coast sat on the front row with the other dignitaries in a metal folding chair under a collapsible canopy set up outside the police station. Chief Carver sat to his left, and next to Carver was DA Cane. Mayor Lyndsay stood at a podium addressing the crowd of about sixty people. Red was conspicuous by his absence.

Rick leaned over toward Dan. "Where the hell is your sidekick?" he asked angrily.

Dan shrugged. "I don't know, I haven't heard from him since six this morning."

"What was he doing then?"

"Watching the Weather Channel, I guess. He called in the middle of the night to tell me it might rain." Dan leaned forward and gazed at the clear-blue sky. "Guess they were wrong again."

"He better get here quick. I told the mayor this was a bad idea."

"Ouch."

"Also," Rick said, "I called CPS about that Tinka woman."

"And?"

"I was right, she is one of Papi's girls."

"One of his girls? How many's he got?"

"Four that I know of. All big earners. According to arrest records, Tinka gets anywhere from six hundred to eight hundred per hour."

"Christ. With that kind of income, no wonder he only needs four girls."

"And it's no wonder he won't let her go. She's tried to get away from him a few times—after her arrests. Even held down legit jobs for a while, but she always ends up going back."

Dan glanced at the mayor and then back at Rick. "How long can he keep those jaws flapping?"

"Hopefully till Red gets here."

Dan gazed out at the crowd for a moment. He made eye contact with Maxine. She smiled and gave him a little wave. He smiled back. His eyes went to Elisa Pena who was seated in the front row between her parents. He glanced up at the sky again. Thick dark clouds were moving in.

"Maybe I'll look into it," said Dan.

"Look into what?" Rick asked.

"Anna Tinka's situation."

"No, you won't."

"I think I should."

"No you shouldn't."

"Why not?"

"Because it will end with a bunch of shit for me to clean up."

"I'm just gonna talk to her."

"Why can't you ever listen to me? Every time you stick your nose—"

"Here he is," Dan said, pointing.

Rick looked up to see Red walking through the crowd with a big grin on his face. He was dressed to the nines in a tasteful suit that fit the big man well, a carnation adorned the double-breasted jacket's lapel. The pineapple print tie was way too loud for the occasion, but Dan had to admit Red had cleaned up nicely. He gazed down at his Dockers and polo shirt—Maxine's suggestion—with a touch of embarrassment.

"About time," Rick said as he reached them.

Red took a seat next to Dan and frowned briefly at his casual attire. "Sorry, I over slept. Then I stopped at Wendy's on my way over. The line at the drive-thru was longer than I thought it would—"

"And without further ado," Lyndsay said, with a dramatic wave of his arm, "may I present to you the two men who rescued little Elisa Pena from the clutches of her captors: Dan Coast and Jim Baxter, or as his friends call him, Red." The mayor stepped back from the podium and began clapping.

The crowd joined in the applause and Dan felt his face flush; he was more embarrassed than he thought he would be. The two men stood and the applause grew louder. Red was grinning from ear to ear.

"They love us," Red said.

Rick stood and shook their hands and smiled for the camera.

"Front page news," said Red.

Dan and Red stepped up to the podium. Mayor Lyndsay stared into the camera as he smiled and handed each man a walnut plaque. "I'm sure I speak for the entire city of Key West when I say thank you, gentlemen, for your incredible act of selflessness and heroism."

Red took his plaque, and pushing in front of Lyndsay, stepped up to the microphone. He tapped the mic twice with the tip of his finger. Just as he was about to speak, the sky grew dark and a flash of lightning cut across the sky. There was a loud crack of thunder. Rain came down like the sky had been ripped open. The crowd scattered. Rick, Lyndsay, and Cane ran for the police station.

Red watched as the parking lot emptied. "Son of a bitch," he said.

"Don't worry, pal," Dan reassured him. "Maybe you'll commit another incredible act of selflessness and heroism one of these days."

Chapter Sixteen

Maxine walked out of the bathroom drying her hair with a towel. "Wow, that was a lot of rain," she said.

Dan stood in the dining room with the palms of his hands resting on the bar top He was staring at the half-empty bottle of tequila he hadn't touched in seven days.

"What are ya doing?" Maxine asked.

"Visiting an old friend," he replied. He turned and leaned back against the bar and took his cell phone out of his pocket. He began flipping through the pictures he had taken in Rick's office. "Rick gave me something to work on."

"That's great. Maybe that'll keep your mind off not drinking."

"Maybe."

"What is it?"

"A murder case from a few years back."

Maxine draped the towel around her shoulders. "Hope it's nothing dangerous."

"Shouldn't be."

"Who was murdered?"

"Some woman a few streets over. Says in the files that her husband was the number one suspect, but they had nothing to go on. Not enough evidence for an arrest."

"When did it happen?"

"March, 2010."

"That's seven years ago. What evidence can you get?"

"I don't know."

"Where will you start?"

"I don't know."

"Sounds like you have everything taken care of," Maxine said, as she walked into the kitchen. "I'm going to make a sandwich. You want a sandwich?"

"I'm not that hungry." Dan reached for his cell phone and dialed.

"Hello?" Rick said.

"Rick, you said the Tinka woman held down a couple jobs after each time she was arrested."

"Yeah."

"What kind of jobs were they?"

"How the hell would I know that?"

"Can you find out for me?"

"Why?" Rick groaned. "I thought you were going to be working on something for me. You asked for something to do and I—"

"Oh, and one other thing, Rick, I was just sitting here making out a check for a large donation to the Key West Police Benevolent Society, and I was wondering who I make that out to."

"You bastard."

"That's not a very nice way to speak to a donor. I was thinking maybe enough to buy some much needed gear, or whatever."

"I'll check and see where she worked."

"Thanks, Rick. You're a real pal."

"Yeah." Rick hung up the phone and Dan grinned proudly.

Maxine stuck her head into the doorway. "Did I just hear you say you were going to donate to the PBA?"

"Yut."

"How much?"

Dan shrugged. "Enough to make a difference, but not so much that they won't need more."

"How much would that be?"

"I'm not sure. Can you look into that for me?"

"If you make a donation to the Maxine Myers Fund."

"On second thought, I'll look into it myself." Dan put his phone back in his pocket and pushed himself away from the bar. He walked across the room to the front door and stared out through the glass panel. "It's getting nice out." he said matter-of-factly.

"Ooh, maybe there'll be a kickball game this afternoon," Maxine replied.

"Don't you have to work?" Dan asked.

Maxine laughed. "Nope, we get to spend the whole day together."

"Good. Cram that sandwich in your gullet and let's go for a walk."

"Where?"

"Around the block. There's a few things I want to check on."

"Maybe after, we could walk downtown?"

"Maybe."

"*Maybe* if we walk downtown we can come back and have sex again."

Dan turned to see Maxine standing in the doorway staring at him with a sexy little grin. "Okay, we can walk downtown," he agreed.

"That's what I thought," Maxine said. "You're not the only one who can get what they want on the promise of a donation."

*****

After Maxine had finished her lunch, she, Dan, and Buddy walked out the front door and started down the street. As they walked along, Maxine reached over and took Dan's hand; they interlocked their fingers. They took a left onto George Street, and then a left onto Patricia. Dan let go of Maxine's hand and reached into his pocket for his phone. He searched through the photo gallery until he came to the picture he was looking for.

"What are you doing?" Maxine asked.

"Looking for an address," Dan replied. He stopped, and zoomed in on the photo.

"Whose?"

"David Maday."

"Who is David Maday?"

"The man who killed his wife back in 2010." Dan scanned the house numbers and names on the mailboxes.

"*Allegedly* killed his wife," Maxine corrected.

"That house right there," said Dan, pointing his finger at a small, one-story block home. A four-foot concrete fence, painted white to match the home, divided the properties on each side and the rear. Set into the fence was a wooden gate with wrought iron inserts fashioned in the shape of a whimsical octopus—this was Key West, after all. The empty driveway was white crushed marble. There were three small palmettos against the front wall and two larger palm trees in the middle of the front yard.

"I'm gonna take a look in the backyard," Dan said.

"What if someone's home?" Maxine asked.

Buddy lay down on the sidewalk at their feet.

"There's no car in the driveway," Dan pointed out. "He's probably at work."

"How do you know he hasn't remarried? Maybe his wife is home."

Dan started toward the gate. "I'm just gonna take a peek."

Maxine looked around the neighborhood nervously.

"You keep a look-out," Dan said. "And grab that dog's collar."

Maxine crouched and took hold of Buddy. "You stay here with me," she said, "while your moronic friend gets arrested for trespassing."

"Arrested? Ha!" said Dan over his shoulder. "I'm a PBA donor."

"Yeah, I don't think that's how that works."

"I think it is." Dan put his hands on top of the gate and stood on his tip-toes.

"What do you see?" Maxine whispered loudly.

"Small yard," Dan replied. "Pool takes up most of it."

"Can I help you?" a man shouted from across the street.

Dan, who was just about to reach over the gate and unlock it, spun around and started back down the driveway.

Buddy let out a loud bark.

"Excuse me, sir," Dan said when he got to the sidewalk. "Don't I know you?"

The old man was in his mid-seventies and carried his lawn rake across the street with him. He lowered his head and peeked out over his Coke bottle glasses. "No, you don't know me," he replied harshly. "Now, what the hell are ya doin' in Dave's yard?"

"Well, I'm a friend of his and—"

"Like shit you are," the old man argued.

"Have you accepted the lord into your—"

"Listen, asshole, I'm about two seconds from goin' back in the house and callin' the police."

Maxine looked on quietly, wondering how her life had taken a sudden turn in which she was now the accomplice in a situation that warranted cop-calling.

"You mean you don't have a cell phone on ya?" Dan asked.

"No."

"Run, Maxine!"

Maxine turned and ran for it, with Buddy and Dan close behind. When they reached the corner Dan looked back to see the old-timer doing his best to keep up. He waved his rake in the air and shouted, "Get back here!"

When Maxine reached Atlantic Boulevard, Dan shouted, "Left, left!"

Maxine turned left.

"Into the condos!" Dan hollered.

Maxine ran up the driveway and into the parking lot of the Atlantic Condominiums. She slowed, and Buddy slowed with her. Dan ran past her and the dog. "He's right behind us!" he panted. Maxine screamed and hauled ass again.

Together they ran past the tennis courts and out onto Bertha Street. They crossed the street and ran into a vacant lot where they took cover behind a block wall. Dan struggled to catch his breath. Maxine wasn't even breathing hard. They sat in the dirt with their backs against the wall.

"Wow, who would have thought that old bastard could hotfoot it after us like that?" said Dan.

"Yeah, who would have thought?" Maxine replied.

Dan grinned. "Fun though, right?"

"What if he gives our descriptions to the police?"

"You worry too much. Did you see how thick Mr. Magoo's glasses were? He ain't giving no description to nobody."

"You know him?"

"Know who?"

"The old man with the rake. You called him Mr. Magoo."

"You know, the nearsighted old guy in the cartoon. Couldn't see a damn thing."

"Sorry, I don't know who that is."

"You're shitting me, right? Mr. Howell from Gilligan's Island did the voice, for chrissakes! Oh, never mind."

"Must be more of your childish nostalgia from the olden days, huh?" said Maxine, smirking.

"Yeah, back when cartoons were good." Dan got up on his knees and looked over the wall for any sign of their pursuer. "I don't see him anywhere."

"Maybe you're as blind as Mr. Magoo."

"Maybe you talk as much as Jabberjaw."

"Who's that?"

"He was a shark who—forget it." Dan got to his feet and brushed off his bare knees. "Let's go home. If I remember correctly, you owe me a roll in the hay."

Maxine pulled herself up using the edge of the wall. "If I remember correctly, we never made it downtown."

"I really need a drink. Where the hell is that dog?"

Chapter Seventeen

Knock, knock.

Dan opened his eyes; it was still dark. He rolled over and looked at the alarm clock on the nightstand: 5:36a.m.

Knock, knock, knock.

Dan rubbed his eyes.

"What was that?" Maxine asked quietly in a raspy morning-voice.

"I think someone's knocking on the door."

"Who would it be at this hour?" Maxine pulled back the covers.

Dan grabbed her arm. "I'll get it," he said. He climbed out of bed and pulled on his boxer shorts that were lying on the floor, next to the bed. "Wait here."

Dan walked bare-foot into the dining room and looked through the glass panel in the front door; there was no one there. He walked into the kitchen and pulled open the back door; no one there, either.

Knock, knock, knock.

Dan looked back over his shoulder. The knocking was coming from the front door. He shut the back door and made his way through the dining room and into the living room. As he walked past the sleeping dog, he shook his head. "Really, dog? You don't hear that?"

Dan turned the knob and slowly opened the front door. Sarah Tinka was looking up at him. He looked past her into the empty street, and then back down at the little girl. "When we said, 'come back anytime,' we didn't mean five thirty in the morning," he informed her.

"My mom never came home last night," Sarah responded.

"Maxine!" Dan hollered.

Maxine rounded the corner into the dining room seconds later. "What's the matter?" she asked.

Dan stepped aside to give her a clear view of the little girl at their door. "We have a visitor."

"Oh my God, it's Sarah! Are you okay?"

"My mom didn't come home last night."

"Come in," Maxine said. She reached over and flipped on the dining room light.

Sarah stepped in and Dan swung the door shut. "I'll make coffee," he grumbled.

Maxine held out her hand to Sarah. "Come and sit on the couch. Tell me what happened."

They got settled and Sarah said, "My mom called me last night to say she would be home in a little while, but she never showed up."

"What time was that?"

"I don't know."

"Were you watching TV?"

"Yes."

"What was on when she called?"

"*Full House*."

"That's on Nickelodeon from nine to eleven," Dan called out.

Maxine smiled and nodded toward the kitchen. "Thanks, Mr. TV Guide."

Sarah smiled back. "I fell asleep after she called."

"Has this ever happened before?"

"No, she's always home in the morning when I wake up."

Buddy got up from his bed and walked over next to Sarah and sat on the floor.

Sarah reached out and scratched his head. "Hi, Buddy," she said. Buddy laid his head on the couch cushion.

"Are you hungry?" Maxine asked. "Did you eat supper last night?"

Sarah continued to stroke the dog's head. "I had mac and cheese for supper."

"Did you make it yourself?"

Sarah nodded. "Yes," she said with pride. "I can make scrambled eggs, and grilled cheese too."

"That's great. Did you make scrambled eggs this morning?"

"No, I didn't eat yet."

"You want me to make you something?"

"Sure … please."

"Dan!"

"On it!" shouted Dan.

Maxine grabbed the remote control and turned on the television.

Dan opened the fridge and grabbed the carton of eggs. "Scrambled okay?" he called out.

"Yes, please," said Sarah.

Twenty minutes later, Dan walked into the dining room with a plate for Sarah, and one for Maxine. He stopped dead in the doorway. "Jesus Christ," he whispered. He stared at the front door.

Maxine and Sarah looked up at Dan and then their eyes went slowly to the front door as well.

Filling the entire glass panel of the door was a behemoth of a man. His head was shaved. He wore a black T-shirt that looked like it had been spray-painted over the bulging muscles of his chest and arms. The huge black man smiled, revealing a gold upper front tooth. Each earlobe displayed a large diamond earring.

"That's my mom's boss," Sarah said.

Never taking his eyes from the door, Dan side-stepped slowly to his left and placed the two plates on the table. He walked gingerly to the door and slowly pulled it open, wishing he had a big club. "Can I help you?" he asked. His voice cracked halfway through the sentence.

"I'm looking for a little girl," the behemoth said. His voice was like the guttural tone of a lion.

Dan cocked his head. "That's just sick," he replied.

"You yankin' my chain?"

"Pal, I probably couldn't lift your chain."

He looked past Dan at Maxine and Sarah seated on the couch. "Come on, Sarah," he said trying to soften his tone. "Your mom's waiting for you in the car."

Dan glanced past the big man at the gray Mercedes parked in the street. Anna Tinka was in the front seat. The window was up and she was bobbing her head to whatever tune was playing.

Sarah didn't move.

"I'm guessing you must be Papi Garcia," Dan said.

"Good guess." His eyes went back to Sarah. "Come on, honey, let's go."

Sarah scooted closer to Maxine

Papi stepped inside and Dan moved to intercept him.

Papi grinned. "Really?"

"Really," Dan replied.

Papi tried to side-step him but Dan aped his movements.

"I don't want to hurt you, little fella," Papi said.

Dan didn't budge. "Then go back to your car and have her mother come in for her."

Papi placed his hand on Dan's chest and effortlessly pushed him back about three feet.

Buddy jumped up from his bed and growled.

"Dan!" Maxine shouted.

Dan moved forward.

"I'm taking her with me," Papi said as he moved toward the couch.

Dan drew back and let Papi have a right to the chin and then a left to the gut.

Papi's head barely moved. He grabbed Dan by the front of the shirt with both hands and tossed him through the air. Dan hit the table near Buddy's bed, knocking Alex's framed picture to the floor; the glass frame shattered against the hardwood.

Buddy leapt at Papi, clamping his jaws tightly on the big man's left bicep. Papi cried out in pain.

Dan jumped to his feet and ran at Papi. Flying through the air, he hit him in the chest with both feet. Papi stumbled backwards onto the porch, through the screen door. Buddy released his grip just as Papi tumbled down the front steps.

"Call 911!" Dan shouted. He turned and ran toward the bedroom. He shoved open the door and dropped to his knees, sliding across the bedroom floor to the nightstand. Yanking open the drawer he reached inside and pulled out his 9mm.

When Dan exited the hallway, Papi Garcia was just charging back into the living room—with Buddy barking behind him—like a rabid bull. He had a wild look in his eyes and the veins on his neck and arms were bulging. "Stop!" Dan shouted.

Papi halted abruptly.

Dan trained the weapon on Papi's billboard-sized chest. "Don't you fucking move," Dan said as calmly as he could, "or I'll empty this clip in you before you take a second step."

Papi slowly raised his hands. "You're making a big mistake, Coast," he said.

"I've made 'em before."

"But you may not live to make them again."

"Please, hurry," Dan heard Maxine say into her phone. He didn't take his eyes off of Papi.

"Maxine, you take Sarah and go into the bedroom and lock the door."

Maxine got up and grabbed Sarah by the hand and did as she was told.

"What now, Coast?" Papi asked.

"We're just gonna stand here and wait till the cops arrive."

"Papi! What's taking you so long?" Anna Tinka shouted from the car.

"You keep your ass in the car!" Papi hollered back over his shoulder. "You hear me?" He returned his attention to Dan. "That 9mm gonna get awful heavy."

"If it does, I'll empty some of the lead."

"You got an answer for everything, white boy."

"That's racist."

Papi smiled. "I'm thinkin' I'm gonna be sad when I kill you."

Dan heard the approaching sirens. Neither man spoke again; they just took each other's measure with eyes that never blinked.

A few seconds later two Key West patrol cars pulled up in front of the house.

"Don't move!" an officer shouted.

Dan went to lay his weapon down on the table, but the table was no longer there. It was in several pieces on the floor, as was the picture frame containing Alex's photograph. Dan crouched down and laid the gun on the floor.

"Get down on your knees," the officer said. "Very slowly."

Papi lowered himself to his knees.

"Now interlock your fingers behind your head."

Papi did as he was ordered.

Dan looked on as the officer cuffed Papi, and then breathed a sigh of relief.

Maxine emerged from the bedroom. Sarah peered around her cautiously.

"Dan, are you okay?" Maxine asked.

Dan slumped against the wall. "Yeah. But I think you'd better bring me a clean pair of shorts."

Chapter Eighteen

Chief Carver slid the key into the handcuffs, releasing the lock. "Are you sure you don't want to press charges, Mr. Garcia?" he asked. They stood in Dan's front yard near a Key West patrol car. Dan stood on the sidewalk, and Maxine was seated on the front steps.

"You gotta be kidding me," Dan said angrily. "Charges for what?"

Pappi Garcia rubbed his wrists and grinned as he stared at Dan. He lifted his arm and inspected the bite mark; there was no blood. "No, I don't think so, Chief. It was all just a big misunderstanding. Ain't that right, Coast?"

"No," Dan replied. "I understood. Understood that you're a giant piece of shit."

"Dan!" Rick scolded.

"It's okay, Chief," Papi said. "Tempers gonna flare in these types of situations. I'm sure in the next few days Mr.

Coast and I will have a long talk about what happened here today, and I'm positive he will apologize for everything."

"I wouldn't be so sure," Dan argued.

Papi looked toward his Mercedes. A female officer was bent over talking to Anna through the passenger side window. Sarah was in the back seat on her knees staring out through the rear window.

"Am I free to go?" Papi asked.

"Yes," Rick replied.

Papi walked toward his car, still rubbing his wrists. When he reached the driver's side door he looked back at Dan. Pretending his hand was a pistol, he let his thumb drop, and faked recoil. He put his finger to his lips and blew away the imaginary smoke. He winked and then climbed into his car.

Rick turned his attention back to Dan. "I don't want any more trouble between you two."

"You better tell *him* that," Dan responded.

They both watched as Papi pulled away from the curb and headed down the street.

"Alright, guys! Let's get out of here!" Rick hollered.

The four other officers climbed back in their cars. Rick wedged his bulk behind the steering wheel of his cruiser and spun his tires as he left.

Dan turned and walked toward his house.

"That was exciting," Maxine said.

"Yeah," Dan replied. He walked up the steps past her and into the house. "Good job, dog," Dan knelt down to pet Buddy's head and then turned his attention to the busted table. He scanned the floor for the photograph of Alex.

"I put it on the table," Maxine said from behind him.

Dan said nothing as he picked up the four or five broken pieces of pine. He carried them through the house and out the back door; Buddy followed. He walked down the gravel path to the fire pit and tossed in the remains of the table. Then he and Buddy walked down to the water. Buddy picked up his tennis ball along the way.

Dan sat Indian-style in the sand watching Buddy splash through the water, as carefree as if nothing happened. After a few minutes Maxine came and sat down beside him. She put her arm through his and rested it on his thigh.

"Did you buy the table when you were together?" Maxine asked softly.

Dan shrugged.

"You can tell me. You can talk about anything with me."

"I know." Dan stared out at a sailboat making a pretty picture on the horizon. "We bought it in Old Forge. We used to go up there three or four times a year ... just for the day. Sometimes we would rent a canoe and take it out on First Lake or sometimes on the Moose River. Afterward we would sit outside at a little bar called Slickers. We'd have a few drinks and listen Paul Case or whoever they had playing guitar and singing that day." Dan raked his fingers through the sand as he spoke. "They had these red Adirondack chairs, and we'd sit there and watch the sunbathers on the beach. We always talked about buying a camp up there. We knew we couldn't afford it, but we would talk about it anyway."

"Sounds nice," said Maxine.

Dan nodded slowly. "It was. One day we were walking along Route 28, where all the little shops are, and Alex spotted that table in a window. She had to have it.

Twenty-five dollars' worth of material in that goddamn table with a $175 price tag on it."

"But you bought it because you loved her."

"I only brought a few things with me when I moved down here. I rented one of the smallest U-Haul trailers they had, and stuffed it with a few of the things that meant something to me."

Dan didn't say anything more about the table. He lay back in the sand with his fingers laced behind his head and stared up at the clear blue sky. After a few minutes he said, "I bought the camp."

"What?" Maxine asked.

"The camp … I bought one just before I came down here. Nothing fancy: a small two-story, two-bedroom log cabin on Third Lake."

"You've never mentioned that."

"I've never mentioned it to anyone. It's right on the water. It's got a little dock to park a boat, and there's a hammock stretched between two huge cedar trees. In the yard there's a small fireplace."

"Sounds really nice," Maxine said.

"It looks nice in the photographs. I've never been there."

Maxine looked down at him. "You've never been there?"

"Nope."

"Who takes care of the place?"

"A guy who lives in town. Every fall he closes it down for the winter, and every spring he opens it up for the summer."

"But it just sits there empty."

"Yup."

Buddy walked over and lay down beside Maxine and pushed his nose up under her hand.

"Thanks for listening," Dan said.

"You're welcome."

"Ya know, the longer I go without a drink, the harder it is to push old memories out of my head."

"I'm here whenever you need me to listen."

"This sucks."

"Alcohol probably kept you keep from dealing with things you should have dealt with a long time ago."

"Probably."

"If you decide you would like to talk to someone, just let me know."

"I'm talking to you now."

"I mean a professional."

"I know what you mean," Dan said. "A prostitute, right?"

"You're an idiot."

"Never said I wasn't."

Chapter Nineteen

"Hey!" Red hollered when Dan walked through the front door of Red's Bar and Grill. "Long time no see."

Dan removed his Wayfarers as he walked into the bar. "You saw me yesterday at the awards ceremony."

Red tossed the bar rag over his shoulder and leaned his big meaty hands on the bar top. "I meant here, touch hole."

Dan climbed aboard his favorite bar stool. "Great speech at the ceremony, by the way."

"Shut up. I figured it would rain. Just my luck. Just about to deliver some words of wisdom to my fans, and boom goes the thunder." Red reached for a rocks glass, filled it with ice and 7UP, dropped in a lime wedge, and pushed it across the bar to his sober friend.

"Your fans?" Dan asked.

"What, heroes can't have fans? I bet Superman has plenty of fans."

"You're comparing yourself to Superman?"

"Yeah. Who knows what would have happened to that little girl if it wasn't for us?"

Dan sipped his soda. "Okay, okay, I guess to that kid and her parents you might be Superman, but to me you're more like one of the X-Men."

Red smiled proudly. "Really? Which one?"

"I dunno. You remind me of so many mutants."

"Bastard! I should have known that wasn't a compliment."

"Yeah, you should have," Dan agreed. "I'm hungry. Can Jocko make me a fish sandwich and fries?"

"Fish sandwich and fries," Red grumbled. "You know how many great seafood dishes are prepared on this island every day, and all you ever seem to order is a fish sandwich."

"I like fish sandwiches."

"Jocko has a special today: Mahi Mahi topped with blue cheese crumbles and baked. He bakes it to perfection, then tops it with a cream sauce of blue cheese, garlic, blackened seasoning, and white wine."

"Wow that sounds really good."

"It's for dinner tonight, but I can have him whip you up one right now, if you'd like."

"I got a better idea," Dan said. "How about if you have him make me a piece of cod, dipped in batter, dropped in really hot grease, and then—here's the kicker—have him throw it on a bun with tartar sauce?"

"Fine," Red said. "Fries too?"

"Of course."

"Sweet potato fries?" Red asked hopefully.

"The man who invented the sweet potato fries should be shot."

"I'll take that as a no." Red disappeared through the kitchen door and Dan heard him holler "Order up!"

When Red returned, Dan was behind the bar making his own second drink. "Get out from behind there," said Red. "I don't need your help."

Dan returned to his seat. "Guess who paid me a little visit this morning."

Red dried one glass after another and placed them on a shelf over the back bar. "I have no idea."

"Papi Garcia."

"Why does that name sound familiar?"

"He's Anna Tinka's pimp."

"Why would he pay you a visit?"

"Sarah showed up at our door early this morning."

"The little girl?"

"Yeah. She said her mother never came home last night. Garcia showed up a little while later with Anna in the car."

Red tossed his rag on the counter and grabbed a coffee mug off the back bar. "And what did you do?" he asked.

"I showed him who was boss."

Red cocked his head. "You showed *him* who was boss? How exactly did you do that?"

Dan reached around and rubbed his own stiff back. "Well, first I hit him with a right, then a left, and then he tossed me across the room like a rag doll."

"When did you show him who was boss?"

"Well, then Buddy attacked him. Which gave me time to get to my gun. Once the 9mm was pointed at his head, he knew who was boss."

"You're a brave man, Dan Coast … I mean as long as you're holding a gun."

"Not real brave, Red. I gotta admit, I think I shat myself a little when he threw me across the room."

Red poured himself a cup of coffee. "Nothing to be ashamed of, my friend."

"That ever happened to you before?" Dan asked his friend.

"God, no. I'm not a little bitch."

"Ouch."

Red sipped his coffee and then chuckled at his own jab. "So when are we gonna look into that old murder case?"

"Already started it."

"Without me? What the hell?"

"Calm down. Maxine and I just walked by the guys house. I wanted to have a look around."

"How did it go?"

Dan thought about the old man with the rake chasing him and Maxine for three blocks. "Uneventful," he replied.

"So, what's next?"

Dan rubbed his stubbly chin. "I'm not sure. Maybe we better meet at my place later and get out the old case board." Dan grinned big when he said case board. The case board was a giant dry erase board on wheels that Dan had purchased almost a year ago during the Henry Davis case. Dan had seen similar boards used in murder cases on some of his favorite cop shows, and felt he needed one as well.

A smile slowly bloomed across Red's face as well. "I love the case board."

"I know you do, pal. I know you do." Dan downed the remainder of his drink. "I emailed you all the pictures I took in Rick's office."

Red looked shocked. "All by yourself?"

"Shut up," Dan responded. "Can you just print them all out and bring them with you when you come to my house?"

"Sure, I can do that. What time you want me there?"

Dan glanced at the clock over the bar. "Be to my place at seven."

"I'll be there."

Dan slid off his stool and headed for the door.

"Hey!" Red called out.

"What?" Dan hollered back, without turning around.

"*Did* you email those pictures to me all by yourself?"

"No. Maxine helped me."

"And what do you want me to do with this fish sandwich Jock is making you?"

"You eat it."

"But I'm not hungry."

"I think we both know that's a lie."

Chapter Twenty

Dan sat on the steps of his front porch sipping a rocks glass filled with ice and Mountain Dew. He had purchased a twelve-pack on his way home from Red's and was now half way through his third can.

The street was quiet and Dan was thankful for that. He wondered if Orrin Stein had gone back to Maine with his family. He wondered what Julian Thompson was doing. He wondered if Sarah Tinka had eaten dinner. He wondered what the Christ was wrong with him that he gave a shit about any of these neighborhood kids. Dan knew he would have to start drinking again eventually. He figured he would start again just before the point where he started taking pictures of rainbows with his cell phone and posting them on Facebook.

Skip's yellow Volkswagen Thing pulled up to the curb. Red and Skip were both mid-laugh. Dan figured one of them had just made a joke about the lonely ex-boozer who sat by himself on an old set of wooden steps. *Is paranoia a symptom of sobriety?* Dan pondered.

"Dan the man!" Skip shouted. "How they hangin', brodiddley?"

Dan didn't answer, he wasn't in the mood for Skip's bullshit.

Red put a foot on the car seat and jumped over the passenger side door to the ground. His large feet kicked up dust like a Clydesdale counting to one. "What's up, pal?" he asked. "Sitting out here with all your friends?"

"Ha!" Skip laughed. "Good one, Red Man."

"Yeah," Dan half-heartedly agreed, "good one."

Skip rounded the car with a red rubber ball tucked under his arm.

"What the Christ is that for?" Dan asked.

"It's a ball," Skip replied.

"I know it's a ball. Why did you bring a ball?"

"I brought it for the kids. I was at Kmart last night and there was a whole bin of 'em, so I grabbed one. I noticed the ball they was using was pretty beat."

"Don't bring the kids gifts, for chrissakes. I'll never get rid of them. You're as bad as Maxine."

"Calm down, brocephus." Skip said, "It's just a ball."

"What are ya drinking?" Red asked.

"Mountain Dew," Dan replied.

"Yuck," said Red.

"That shit'll kill ya," Skip said. "You'd be better off going back to the booze, my man. I got myself hooked on the Dew about five years back. Let me warn ya, it's a bad monkey to shake."

"Thanks for the warning," Dan replied. He held up the glass and shook the ice. "I think it's pretty good."

Skip started up the steps and slapped his friend on the back. "It's liquid crack. Now let's solve ourselves a murder."

Dan gave Red a why-did-ya-bring-*him* look; Red just shrugged his shoulders.

When Dan and Red came through the door, Skip was already rolling the case board into the middle of the living room. He looked to Red. "Where's those photographs, Red Man?" he asked.

Red spun on his heels. "Oops! Left them in the car."

Skip grabbed a red marker from the tray below the board. "Okay, what name should we give this case?"

Dan snatched the marker from Skip's hand. "I'll do the writing, if you don't mind."

"Awe, come on, dude. I want to write something."

"Then get your own case board."

"Maybe I will. Maybe I'll get a board and start solving crimes myself, and put you out of business."

"I'm not in business," Dan reminded the surfer-like man-child.

"Oh yeah."

"Here they are," Red announced as he walked back through the door. He held the photos out in front of him. Skip reached for them, but Dan was quicker.

"Really, dude!" said Skip. "This is so bogus. What are ya gonna let me do?"

Dan had long nursed a sneaking suspicion that Skip wasn't really the stoner/doofus he played to perfection. But one thing was for sure: he was more irritating than a tick on your bunghole.

Dan pointed at his empty glass on the dining room table. "Fix me another drink."

"Yeah," said Red. "Make me one just like his, only add some Scotch to the Mountain Dew."

"I don't have any Scotch," Dan informed him.

"Add some whiskey."

"Nope," Dan said as he shuffled through the photographs.

"Tequila."

Dan jerked his head toward the bar where a half empty bottle sat, still calling his name, but not as loud.

"Coming right up," Skip said.

"What should we call this case?" Dan asked.

Skip shot him a look.

"How about Cold Case Number One?" Red offered.

"Not very catchy," Dan said.

"It's gotta have the words cold and case in there," Red said. "Cold case just sounds cool."

Dan scratched his chin as he thought, putting a thick red line from the marker across his cheek. "How about Dave and Elizabeth Maday's Cold Case?" Dan looked at the tip of the red marker and then at Red. "Did I just put a red mark on my face?"

Red inspected Dan's face. "Nope," he lied. "Who's Dave and Eliza—"

"Elizabeth is the woman who was murdered."

"Oh, then that sounds good."

Skip returned with the drinks and set them on the table. "Order up," he said.

Dan wrote DAVE AND ELIZABETH MADAY'S COLD CASE at the top of the board, and then stepped back to admire his work. He turned around. "What do you think?"

Skip pointed at his own cheek.

"What?" Dan asked.

"You got a big red mark on your cheek."

"Red, you bastard," said Dan

Red snickered. "Time's a wastin'. Put the photos on the board, Danno."

"Can I do it?" Skip asked.

"Sure," Dan said.

Skip hurried forward like a teacher's pet being asked to solve a problem on the chalkboard. He took the seven printouts from Dan and placed them one at a time into the clip magnets and stuck them to the case board. Three of the photographs were of police paperwork and the other four were crime scene photos. He stepped back and looked at his two friends. "There!" he said proudly.

They all three stared at the board.

"Good job," Dan said. "Remind me to put a gold star next to your name."

"Now what?" Red asked.

Dan shrugged.

"Should we get a game of kickball going?" Skip asked.

Dan and Red ignored him.

"It's still kinda light out," Skip added.

"Shut up," Dan said. He sighed loudly. "Okay, according to the police report, Dave Maday reported his wife missing on June 14 2010, a little before midnight; it was a Monday."

Dan stepped forward and drew a time line across the board and filled in the date and day, and wrote WIFE REPORTED MISSING.

"Suspects?" Red asked.

"The husband was questioned as well as a male coworker of Elizabeth's."

"Boyfriend?" Skip asked.

"It doesn't say that, but let's assume it was," said Dan. "The guy's name was Franco Rubino."

"Why would we assume the guy was her boyfriend?" Red asked.

"Because the husband was fifty-one and Elizabeth was thirty-two," Dan explained. "Maybe she wanted to dance the wango tango with someone who can still get it up."

"Maxine's a lot younger than you," Skip pointed out.

"Shut up, Skip," Dan said.

"Franco Rubino," Red repeated slowly and rolled his Rs like Ricardo Montalban. He walked in closer to the photos of the police notes and scanned each one. "Aren't there any notes on the conversation between the police and the boyfriend?"

"If there are, they weren't in Rick's folder."

"So all we have to go on is some photographs, the original police report, and a few of the detective's notes," Red said.

"Can we talk to the lead detective?" Skip asked.

"Nope," Dan replied. "Rick doesn't want anyone to know we're working on this."

"Doesn't that make it a little impossible to solve this, dude?" Skip asked.

"Where did Mrs. Maday work?" Red asked.

"Key West Mutual," Dan replied.

"How about the husband?"

"Southern Most Pool and Spa."

"Boom!" Skip hollered and clapped his hands together. "There's a pool in the crime scene photos, right? She's buried under the pool. Case closed."

Dan answered with a mounting slow burn, "Tell me, Shitlock, how could he bury her under a pool that was already there?"

"Oh, yeah."

"Elizabeth's boss said she called in sick that morning around six-thirty," Dan read from the notes. "Dave confirmed that call, and said he kissed her good bye and left for work around eight."

"And that's the last time he saw her?" asked Red.

"Last time anyone saw her," Dan replied.

"If she left the house, someone saw her after that," said Skip. "They might not know it, but someone saw her."

"We don't know that she did leave the house," Dan argued. "On her own, I mean."

"Should we talk to the boyfriend?" asked Red.

"We can't," Dan answered.

"We've gotta talk to someone," said Red. "These few notes and photos aren't enough to solve this case."

"True that, Red Man," said Skip. "I've binge-watched *Cold Case* with that smokin' hot MILF Kathryn Morris. I can't believe this would be everything in the case file."

"Yeah," Dan agreed. "It's like Rick doesn't really want us to solve—son of a bitch."

Red and Skip turned to their friend. "What?" asked Red.

"I bet Rick *doesn't* want us to solve this," said Dan. "I bet he took a bunch of shit out of the folder before he showed it to us. He just did this to get me off his back. That bastard."

Skip chuckled. "Kinda funny though."

"What are we gonna do?" Red asked.

"We're gonna solve this goddamn case," Dan said. "And we'll talk to whoever the hell we want."

"We'll show him," Red added.

"We should think about this over a quick game of kickball," Skip suggested.

"Shut up, Skip," Dan and Red said in unison.

Chapter Twenty-One

Dan awoke at seven-thirty the next morning to the sound of his cell phone alarm. He rolled over and shut it off.

"Going for a run?" Maxine asked.

"Yut," Dan replied.

"How are you feeling?"

Dan searched through his drawer for a T-shirt. "A lot better."

"See, it just takes a while."

"Nine days," Dan said.

"One day at a time," said Maxine.

"Loved that show."

"What show?"

Dan had a vision of Valerie Bertinelli when she was young and cute. "Never mind."

"You want me to come with you?"

Dan pulled a vintage black Ozzy Osbourne: No More Tours T-shirt from 1992 over his head. "Maybe tomorrow."

"Sounds good." Maxine rolled over and pulled the blankets up over her shoulder. "Love you," she said, as Dan walked out of the bedroom.

"Back at ya," Dan returned, with a wave over his shoulder. "Back in a bit."

As Dan ran along, he breathed in deep through his nose and exhaled through his mouth. This morning's run was much easier than his first run a week ago. His breathing was more controlled and the cadence of his stride was more uniform and easier to maintain. He felt better than he had in years. He wondered why he drank at all, but at the same time couldn't wait for the next time he did, and even wondered how long he should keep this sobriety thing up. How long would it take to prove to himself that he drank because he wanted to, not because he had to? How long does it take a sober man's brain to convince him of that lie?

Dan rounded the corner onto Patricia Street. He stared at Dave Maday's house as he rounded the next corner. A car was in the driveway and the lights were on in the house. Dan glanced over at the home of the old man who had chased him and Maxine with the rake; his lights were on as well.

Dan pulled his cell phone out of his pocket and shoved it into the waistband of his shorts. Then he stepped purposely—just in case anyone was watching—at the edge of the sidewalk where it met the grass. He tumbled onto Maday's front lawn, making sure to grind his knees and shoulder into the grass for optimum lawn staining. Dan got up and fake-limped to Maday's front door, knocking three times.

"Can I help you?" Dave Maday asked, when he opened the door. He was wearing blue flannel pajama bottoms and a white T-shirt. His bed head hair was white and so was the two day stubble on his chin and cheeks. His eyes went from Dan to the street and then back to Dan.

"I saw your light on," Dan explained. "I was running and took a little spill." Dan showed Maday the green grass stain on his elbow. "I don't have my cell phone with me, and I was wondering if I could use your phone to call someone to pick me up. I twisted my ankle."

Maday peered out into the street again and then pulled the door open all the way. "Sure," he said. "Come on in."

"Thanks."

"House phone's right there on the stand," Maday said.

"Thanks." Dan picked up the phone and stared at the cradle.

"Something wrong?" Maday asked.

"Yeah, actually. I don't know her number," Dan explained. "She's in my contacts, on my cell phone, but I've never really dialed her number before."

Maday chuckled. "Damn cell phones," he said. "I'll tell you what. Let me throw on some clothes and I'll run you home myself."

"Thanks, that would be great."

"I just made a fresh pot of coffee. Can I make you a cup?"

"Yes, please," Dan replied. "That would be great."

When Maday left the room Dan began looking around. He was standing in the living room and slowly did a complete 360. The room was lime green with white ranch casings around the doors and windows. There were no curtains on the windows, only mini blinds. There was a gas fire place to the right of the front door.

"Cream and sugar in that?" Maday called out from the kitchen.

"Yes, please," Dan said. He didn't use cream or sugar in his coffee, but he figured he might as well keep the homeowner busy as long as he could. *I wonder if I should have him whip me up some eggs?* Dan thought.

Dan walked over to the wooden fireplace mantel, a reclaimed railroad tie adorned with bric-a-brac and several photographs of a stunning young woman arranged with shrine-like devotion. Dan recognized Elizabeth from the photo on the dry-erase board. A wedding photo situated between two brass candlesticks caught his eye: Dave and his young bride, their faces beaming with love and devotion. Just as Alex and Dan looked in their wedding photos.

Above the mantel hung a painting of Elizabeth. Dan couldn't blame Dave for having commissioned it; she was a beautiful woman. She sat on the floor in front of this very same fireplace with her bare legs pulled up under her. Her long red hair cascaded over her shoulders, and a Hollywood smile lit up her freckled face. She was dressed only in a man's white dress shirt. The top three buttons were undone, revealing the sides of her breasts and the space between them. Mesmerized, Dan stared at the painting, trying to wrap his brain around why a vivacious woman like Elizabeth—and Alex—had to die so young.

"That's Elizabeth," Maday said when he entered the room. "She's my wife."

"Dan turned. "Oh, is she at work?" he asked.

Maday handed Dan his cup of coffee. "No. She … passed away a few years ago."

"I'm sorry for your loss," Dan responded. "How did it happen?"

Maday sipped his own coffee as he gazed at the painting. He didn't answer the question.

"I don't mean to pry," Dan said. "It's just that … I lost my own wife a few years back … almost four years ago now."

"It's a terrible tragedy to lose a spouse," Maday said. "There's no pain like it."

"It was a car accident," Dan said. "My Alex, I mean."

Maday took a deep breath. "Elizabeth disappeared a little over ten years ago." He exhaled.

Dan raised an eyebrow. "Disappeared?" he asked. "What do you mean?"

"I came home from work and she wasn't here. I thought she had gone for a walk or something." Maday continued to stare through the painting. "I made dinner. She didn't come home, I tried her cell phone a few times. She didn't answer. It got later, and later, so I called the police to report her missing."

"But they never found her."

"No."

"Then how do you know she's—"

"Ten years and nothing," Maday said. He suddenly snapped out of his trance-like state. "Any way, let me get dressed and I'll run you home."

"Okay, sure," Dan responded.

Maday turned and walked down his hallway.

Dan's eyes went back to the painting. He side-stepped to the right, and then to the left as Elizabeth's eyes, as green as the sea, followed his every movement. He reached into his waistband, pulled out his cell phone, and snapped a picture of the painting.

Chapter Twenty-Two

Dave Maday pulled his black Chrysler 300 to the curb in front of Dan's house. During their drive over, Dan had told Dave a few more things about Alex, and Dave, in return, did the same about his wife.

"There you go," Dave said. "Curbside service."

Dan held out his hand and Dave shook it. "Thanks, Dave," Dan said. "I really appreciate this."

"No problem."

Dan opened the door and climbed out of the car. He turned and bent over to look back inside. "Ya, know, Dave, if you ever want to get together, have a drink, or just talk, give me a call. Might be nice to talk with someone who's been through the same thing."

Dave smiled. "Maybe I'll do that, Dan," he replied.

Dan shut the door, turned, and limped up the sidewalk to his front door. Dave drove off.

Maxine was watching out the front door. "Are you okay?" she asked, stepping out onto the porch. "What happened?"

Dan looked down the street and watched Dave steer his car around the corner. He looked back at Maxine and stopped limping. "I'm fine," he assured her.

"Who was that that dropping you off?"

"*That* … is my new friend Dave. He lives a few blocks over."

Maxine folded her arms in front of her and stared down the steps at her boyfriend. She remained silent, knowing there was some bullshit story coming.

"Seems he lost his wife a few years back," Dan explained. "The police never recovered her body."

"How sad," said Maxine. "And how exactly did you meet your new friend Dave?"

"I took a little tumble in front of his house, so I went to the door to see if I could use his phone to call you."

"Uh-huh. Why didn't you call me?"

"I couldn't remember your number, having never dialed it from a land line."

"Uh-huh. Why didn't you just use your cell phone?"

"I didn't have it with me," Dan replied, as he pulled his cell phone from his waistband.

"Uh-huh. How convenient. No sign of the old rake-wielding neighbor?"

"Nope." Dan started up the steps and walked past Maxine into the house. "Any way, I told him that I too had lost my wife, and we're gonna have a beer together soon and talk about it."

"You're evil."

Dan turned. "Evil? Why do you say that?"

"You're using the death of that poor man's wife to use him and trick him into giving you information about the case."

"Poor man? If that shit bag murdered his wife, he'll get no sympathy from me." He turned back and headed for the coffee maker, kicking off his running shoes halfway across the living room. He glanced down at Buddy's empty bed, and then where the table with Alex's photograph used to be. He turned his head and glared at the half-empty bottle of tequila that sat on the bar against the dining room wall. Dan could hear the bottle calling his name just as loud as it ever had. *Screw you*, he thought. *Not today either*.

Maxine followed Dan into the kitchen. "I thought you said Rick didn't want you speaking to the husband," she said.

"Yeah, so?" Dan responded.

"You told him you wouldn't."

"I lied."

"He's going to be pissed."

"Until I solve this." Dan spun back and grabbed a mug out of the cupboard and poured his coffee. He blew in it and took a sip. "Hey! What flavor is this?"

"Coconut."

"I like it." He drank some more. "Why haven't you ever bought this before?"

"Because you hate flavored coffee."

"Until now." Dan went to another cupboard and got the Pop-Tarts. He opened a package and dropped two of them into the toaster. "You want a Pop-Tart?" he asked.

"I'll pass," Maxine replied.

"I think Rick pulled a bunch of paperwork out of the Maday's case file before he showed it to me."

"Why would he do that?"

"Because he didn't really want me to solve it. He just wanted me off his back for a while."

Maxine chuckled.

"That's not funny," Dan said.

"It's kinda funny," Maxine argued.

"Whatever." Dan's breakfast popped up and he placed them on a plate. He carried the plate along with his coffee down the gravel path that led to the two Adirondack chairs next to the fire pit. He sat down in one of the chairs and set his coffee in the dirt next to him. Shit, he thought. "Maxine!"

Maxine appeared at the back door. "What?"

"Would you bring me the newspaper?"

She didn't answer, she just turned and disappeared.

"Is that a yes?" Dan hollered. His eyes went to the Border Collie watching him from Bev's deck. Buddy was eyeing him between the railing spindles. "Pop-Tart, dog!" Dan shouted, as he waved one of the toaster treats in the air.

Buddy jumped to his feet and ran to his master.

Dan broke off a corner of one of the Pop-Tarts and fed it to Buddy.

Buddy sat and stared at Dan.

"That's all," Dan informed him. "This is *my* breakfast."

The backdoor swung open and Red walked down the steps with Dan's morning newspaper tucked into his armpit.

"Morning, pal!" Red called out.

"What's up?" Dan asked.

"Came by to see if you wanted to get breakfast somewhere."

"I already cooked myself breakfast," Dan answered, pointing at his plate.

"Yum," Red said, and took a seat in the other chair. He handed the paper to Dan.

"Thanks." Dan dropped the paper on the ground next to his cup.

"What's next?" Red asked.

"I'll probably poop and then take a shower."

"I mean with the Mayday case."

"It's Muh-day."

"Okay. What's next with the Muh-day case?"

Dan took a bite of his Pop-Tart. "We need to talk with the boyfriend."

"What about the husband?"

"I spoke with him this morning."

"Without me?"

"I'll fill you in later," Dan explained. "We have to figure out a way to speak to the boyfriend without him getting suspicious. We don't want it to get back to Rick that we're doing just what he told us not to do."

"We got an address on Mr. Rubino?"

"Yeah, if he still lives where he lived ten years ago."

"Maybe it's time for a stakeout."

"Good idea."

"I love stakeouts."

"I know you do." Dan took another bite of his Pop-Tart and tossed the remainder to Buddy. "Shall we go get some breakfast?"

"I could eat," Red replied.

Dan got up from his chair and walked toward the house, with Buddy and Red close behind. "Maxine!" Dan hollered. The trio went from the kitchen into the living room. "Maxine!"

"What?" she hollered.

"We're going to breakfast. You want to come?"

The bathroom door opened a crack. "I'm getting ready for work."

Dan went down the hall and kissed her on the lips through the opening in the door. "I'll see ya later then."

"Didn't you just eat breakfast?"

"The Pop-Tarts? That was just a snack. Besides, all this jogging really builds up an appetite."

"Yeah, I bet," said Maxine. They kissed again and she shut the door.

Dan walked back into the living room, Red was inspecting the case board.

"Franco Rubino's address is 3524 Duck Avenue," Red said. "Are we staking it out in my car or yours?"

"Is yours fixed?" Dan asked.

"No, but I'm driving the Volkswagen Bug."

"We're not using a pink car for a stakeout." Dan held the front door open and Red walked through and down the steps.

"Yeah, you're right. Might be a little conspicuous."

"Wow!" Dan said, letting the screen door slam shut behind him. "Pulled that word out of your ass. Where did you learn a big word like conspicuous?" Dan chuckled to himself.

"I learned it from your mother." Red pulled open the passenger side door of Dan's Porsche and climbed in.

"Ooh … good one."

"Yeah, your mother said that too, after I got done—"

"Okay, okay, that's enough."

"She said that too," Red whispered quickly.

Chapter Twenty-Three

Later that night, after dark, Dan and Red sat across the street, and about two houses down, from 3524 Duck Avenue. Red had called a friend of his at the DMV and found out that Franco Rubino did indeed still live at that address. He also found out that Rubino drove a red 2015 Volvo wagon; that wagon was parked in the driveway. Rubino was five-eleven, had black hair, brown eyes, and he was forty years old—putting him in his early thirties at the time of Elizabeth's disappearance.

Dan sat in the driver's seat with the top down and Red sat next to him. A pair of binoculars sat on the console between them. Dan's Nikon camera sat in his lap.

"Nice night," Red commented.

"Yup," Dan replied. "Except for the mosquitoes."

A plastic Winn-Dixie grocery bag sat on the floor between Red's feet. He reached into it, fiddled with the lid of a cardboard package, and pulled out a white powdered donut. "Want one?" he asked Dan. "It's Hostess. Finger-lickin' good."

Dan glanced over. "No … thanks."

Red took a bite of the donut and powdered sugar fell on the front of his blue Hawaiian shirt, and into the lap of his camouflage cargo shorts.

"Don't get that shit all over my car," Dan said.

"It's just sugar," Red replied. He jammed his big hand back into the bag and pulled out a bottle of Yoo-hoo. He twisted off the top and guzzled down half the bottle.

"Jesus Christ! Have you ever gone more than twenty minutes without eating?"

"I doubt it." Red popped the last of the donut into his mouth, and chased it down with more of his chocolate drink.

"How can you drink that shit?" Dan asked.

"It's good."

"It's chocolate water."

"Yeah, that's what makes it great. You put chocolate in front of anything and it becomes awesome. Chocolate Easter bunny, chocolate milk, chocolate cake, Choco Taco, choc—"

"Okay, okay, I get it, Bubba."

"—and chocolate water."

Dan saw headlights in his rear view mirror. "What the Christ is *he* doing here?"

Red spun his head. "Who?"

"Skip."

"Oh, yeah. I told him we were gonna be on a stakeout tonight."

"And you thought a bunch of cars sitting out front of this guy's house wouldn't be *conspicuous*?"

"Good word, isn't it?" Red grinned.

"Yeah," Dan grumbled. "The only thing that would make it better is if it was *chocolate* conspicuous."

The headlights shut off and Skip leapt over his door. His size twelve Vanns sneakers hit the dirt with a thud. "What's up, bromosapiens?" he asked. Skip put the palms of his hands on the side of Dan's car and catapulted himself into the back seat.

Red held up his grocery bag. "Donut, Skip?" he asked.

"Don't mind if I do, Red Man," Skip replied. He wiggled around trying to get comfortable in the tiny back seat. His ass was in the driver's side seat, and he was turned sideways with his feet in the passenger side seat. His shoulders were wedged in between the front and back seats. "Damn, these seats aren't very comfortable."

Dan grabbed the binoculars and focused them on the front picture window of Rubino's house.

"Any sign of the subject?" Skip asked. He coughed and powdered sugar hit the back of Dan's seat.

"Nothing yet," Red replied.

"How long you guys been here?"

"Twenty minutes."

"Seems a lot longer," Dan grumbled.

Skip dropped his donut and it rolled under the seat. "Oh, shit." He reached under and felt around for it. "Hey, you know there's a bottle of tequila under here?" He hoisted the bottle over the console for Dan's perusal.

"Of course I know there's a bottle of tequila under there," Dan replied. "I put it there. Now, put it back."

Skip stealthily removed the cap, took a big swig, replaced the cap, and put it back where he found it.

"Can we listen to some music?" Red asked.

"No," Dan replied. He continued to stare at the window.

"This is boring."

"Shove another donut in your face," said Dan.

"You want another one, Skip?" Red asked.

"You know it, Red Man," Skip replied. "Got another one of those yoo-hoos?"

"Comin' right up." said Red.

"Car!" Skip whispered loudly.

Dan and Red slouched down in their seats and Skip ducked behind Dan's head rest as a white Subaru Forester whipped into Rubino's driveway and parked behind the Volvo.

"Who's that?" Red asked.

"How the hell would I know?" Dan responded.

All three watched like hawks as a man in his mid-thirties climbed from the car and walked to the door. He knocked three times and stepped back.

Rubino answered the door. He smiled big. The two men put their arms around each other and kissed passionately on the lips.

"Um, I'm starting to think Rubino and Maday's wife weren't lovers," Skip said matter-of-factly.

"I think Rubino's gay," Red added.

"Gee, ya think? What was your first clue?" Dan asked.

"I wish we could hear what they're saying," said Skip.

The two men broke their embrace and went inside, closing the door behind them. After another ten minutes the front picture window went dark.

Dan laid the binoculars back on the center console. "Give me one of those donuts," he ordered.

Red laughed like a mad scientist when he handed Dan the donut. "Now you're one of us."

"Shut up and give me the donut."

"You think Rick knew this guy was gay?" Skip asked.

Dan shrugged his shoulders. "Who knows?" he replied with a mouthful of cakey goodness and powdered sugar. All Dan could think about was washing it down with a big swig of the tequila that lay under the seat.

"Where to now?" Red asked.

Dan started the car. "Let's run by Anna Tinka's place," he answered.

"Sounds good to me," said Skip.

"What about your car?" Red asked.

Dan put the Porsche in gear.

"Oh, yeah," Skip said. He jumped out of the car as the wheels stated rolling. "I'll follow you guys over."

Dan spun the tires, kicking dust and gravel all over Skip's legs and brand new Vanns.

"Hey!" Skip shouted. "Not cool, bro."

Red and Dan chuckled as they drove down the street.

Dan took a left onto Sky View Street and slowed as he drove past the Tinkas' ranch house. It was a few minutes after eleven and the house was dark. Parked in the driveway was Anna's Mini-COOPER, and behind it was parked Papi Garcia's Mercedes.

"One big happy family," Dan said.

"Whatever works for them," Red commented.

"What works for them might not be working for that little girl."

"Who are we to judge?"

"That's what ostriches say right before they stick their heads in the sand." Dan sped up. "I'll drop you back at the bar."

"You gonna come in … for a soda?"

"I don't think so," Dan replied. He glanced at the rear view mirror, Skip was right behind them. "Your buddy will have a drink with you."

"Come in for one," Red pressed.

"I don't know."

Red reached into the plastic bag and pulled out another donut. "Last one," he announced. "You want it?"

"Christ, no," said Dan. "What if you starved to death between here and the bar? I wouldn't want that on my conscience."

"We're only a couple blocks away," Red joked. "I can make it."

"Nope. Go ahead."

Red shoved the whole donut into his mouth with the tip of his index finger.

Dan shook his head. "Good God. It's a good thing that's the last one. Two more and I'd need a giant shoe horn to get you out of the car."

"Fwaterver," said Red with his mouth full.

Chapter Twenty-Four

Dan pulled into Red's Bar and Grill for only the second time in almost two weeks, and backed into a parking spot on the far side of the lot. Skip pulled in right next to him.

"Nothing's changed," Dan said.

"That's not true," Red said. "I put new cakes in the urinals day before yesterday."

The three men walked across the parking lot and through the front door. Cindy Leonard was behind the bar, as usual. Derrick White, Cindy's boyfriend, stood at the old Wurlitzer trying to decide on just the right song. Fifteen or twenty other guests littered the room; a few perched on the orange bar stools, and the others sat at tables.

"Table or bar?" Skip asked.

Dan looked over at his favorite bar stool; an old man in his seventies was sitting on it and nursing a draft beer.

"Might as well grab a table," he said. "Looks like someone has already claimed my seat."

"Move your feet, lose your seat," said Red. "Grab that table over there and I'll get us something to drink."

Dan and Skip went toward a four top near the jukebox, and Red went to the bar.

Dan sat with his back to the wall, facing the door, and Skip sat to his left.

Derrick finally decided on "Wonderful World, Beautiful People" by Jimmy Cliff.

Dan began tapping his fingers on the edge of the table to the beat of the music. "Nice choice," Dan said to Derrick as he passed their table on his way back to the bar.

"You know it, mon," Derrick responded in his best faux Jamaican accent.

"How many days since your last drink?" Skip asked.

"I'd rather not talk about it," Dan replied.

"Oh-*kay*," said Skip. "Then let's talk about why we drove by Anna Tinka's place."

"How did you know that was her house?"

"I told you, I dated a friend of hers once."

"This friend, was she also a friend of Papi Garcia's."

"Sure was. That's why we broke up."

"She a dancer?"

"Among other things."

"What do you mean?"

"I knew she was a dancer, that's how I met her, but a few weeks into it, I found out she was also hooking."

"*Eesh.*"

"Yeah, *eesh*. Needless to say, I dumped her, got the necessary medical tests done, and went on with my life."

"She still around?"

"No, dude. She moved back to Jersey about a year later. Last I heard of her."

"She ever talk to you about Garcia?"

"Just that she was one of his girls. At first I got a little mental, thought about doing the valiant thing and going aggro on his ass, but then I came to my senses."

"Probably a smart decision. He's the size of a house."

"I think I could've held my own."

"Yeah," Dan said. "Held your own ass on the way to the emergency room."

"Here ya go," Red said. He placed Skip's Scotch and soda in front of him, and served Dan his 7UP and lime. "Drink up. But remember, pal, you're driving."

"Funny," said Dan.

Red sat down across from Dan and sipped his rum and Coke. "What are we talking about?"

"Papi Garcia and Anna Tinka," Skip replied. "Dan thinks he's gonna save that little family unit."

"I'm not saving anyone, but Rick said she's tried to get away from that behemoth a few times in the past, and I think if she wants out, we should help her."

"If she wanted out, she would have stayed out," Red offered.

"Sometimes people don't have a choice, Red Man," Skip pointed out. His eyes went back to Dan. "So, how we gonna do this, bromigo?"

"I'm just gonna ask her if she needs my help," Dan stated.

Skip nodded. "Sounds like a straight forward plan."

"What if she says she doesn't need your help?" Red asked.

"Then I'll probably help her anyway."

"That'll piss off Papi Garcia," Skip said.

"I don't care," said Dan.

"How are we gonna help her?" asked Red.

"We'll cross that bridge when we get there."

Red smacked his palms on the table. "Okay, anyone besides me eating?" he asked. "I'm gonna have Jocko fix me something."

"You just ate a bag of donuts," Dan pointed out.

"Large fries here," Skip ordered.

Red looked across the table at Dan. "You?"

"Fish sandwich and fries," Dan replied.

"Surprise, surprise." Red got up and went through the swinging doors and into the kitchen.

The entrance door opened and Dan looked over. In walked Michael Lord and a male friend. Their eyes met, and Dan waived him over.

"Daniel Coast!" Michael sang out. He sashayed to the table with a companion in tow. "What brings you out? Word on the street has it that you quit drinking."

"Where did you hear that?" Dan asked.

"Small island," answered Michael. "And you know I never reveal my sources."

Michael's friend stood quietly behind him. The man was six feet tall, and his button-up shirt was working overtime trying to contain his massive biceps. His shirt open almost to the naval, showcasing his thick, graying chest hair.

"Can I get you a drink at the bar, Mikey?" the big man asked.

"Yes, Todd, please," Michael replied.

Todd turned and went to the bar.

"Mikey?" Dan asked.

Michael rolled his eyes. "I've asked him not to call me that in front of my friends," he said. Michael's eyes went to Skip; he held out his hand. "Haven't we met before, surfer boy?" he said with a little flirtatious lilt to his voice.

"Yo," Skip replied. "A little over a year ago at Dan's Christmas party." Skip took Michael's hand and gave it a little shake.

"Oh, that's right. You assisted Daniel in rescuing a friend of mine. Now I remember. Poor man could have been murdered if you gentlemen hadn't—"

"Michael," Dan interrupted, "do you know a man by the name of Franco Rubino? He's forty years old, dark hair, brown eyes, stands about five-eleven."

Michael gave Dan a sly grin. "Why are you asking, Daniel?"

"I … uh, I was just wondering," Dan stuttered.

"Daniel, would this man happen to be gay, by any chance?"

"Um, yeah, now that you mention it, I believe he is gay."

"And … you think that all gay men know each other?"

"No. I just thought that maybe—"

"With an island full of gay men, am I your only gay friend, Daniel?" Michael asked. He was still wearing the grin.

"Yes."

"That's very offensive, Daniel," Michael said. "Do you assume all black men know each other?"

"Um … I … no."

Michael motioned toward Skip. "Do you think that all sexy young surfer boys know each other?"

"Well, they probably—"

"Yes, I know him," Michael finally admitted.

Skip laughed out loud.

"Then why did you put me through that, dammit?" Dan asked.

"It's fun to watch you squirm, Daniel."

Todd returned holding a hurricane glass in each hand. "Here's your drink, Mikey," said Todd, handing the frozen daiquiri to his date.

Michael took the glass and put the straw in his mouth. He sucked, and then pressed his thumb against his forehead. "Brain freeze, brain freeze," he announce loudly. "Why do frozen drinks have to be so dang cold?"

"If they weren't cold—"

"I'm joking, Todd."

"So, what can you tell me about Rubino?" Dan asked.

"Not much," replied Michael. "I know he's a big shot at some insurance company."

"He's in a relationship with Calvin Lee," Todd added.

Michael turned to his date with a smirk. "And just how do you know that, Todd."

Todd grinned slyly. "I have my ways, Mikey."

Michael moved closer to Todd and snuggled up under his arm. He rubbed Todd's belly. "You sure do." The two men stared into each other's eyes and giggled.

Dan looked toward the ceiling and groaned. "Good God. Someone get the garden hose."

"Don't be jealous, Daniel," Michael said. "You had your chance." Michael stared at Dan and provocatively shifted the straw around in his mouth.

Todd squeezed Michael harder. "He's all mine now," he said.

Skip slapped Dan on the back. "Too bad for you, dude. Michael seems like quite a catch."

"Shut up, Skip," Dan said.

Michael winked at Skip. "Why, thank you, surfer boy."

Red joined the group and stood next to the table. "Food's ready when you guys are," he announced.

"I'm ready," Skip said.

"I'm more than ready," Dan said.

Red turned. "I'll grab the plates."

Dan looked back at Michael. "Any way, the reason I was asking about Rubino is because I'm working on a case that involves the disappearance of a female friend of his—Elizabeth Maday. She disappeared about ten years ago. Do you remember hearing anything about that?"

"Ten years ago? No. I was still in Texas ten years ago," Michael answered. He looked up at Todd. "Does that name ring a bell with you, sweetheart?"

Todd bit his bottom lip and nodded his head. "Yes, it does," he said. "It was front page news and all over the television for weeks. They never found the body, if I remember correctly."

"That's right," said Dan. "Never found the body, and no one was ever charged."

"Most people thought it was the husband," said Todd. "I think I heard he moved away a short time later."

"No, he still lives on the island," Dan said.

"I'm friends with a couple of Rubino's friends," Michael said. "If you would like, I could ask a few questions."

"That would be great," said Dan. "But ask them matter-of-factly, and try not to raise any suspicions."

"I can be very discreet, Daniel."

"Um, okay. You two have a nice evening."

"We will, Daniel, and you tell Maxine I said hello."

"I'll do that." Dan turned to Skip just as Red set his plate in front of him. "I would never have guessed Michael was a Texan."

"Why's that?" Red asked.

"No accent," Skip said.

"Yeah," Dan agreed. "No accent."

Chapter Twenty-Five

When Dan got home, Maxine's car was already in the driveway. Dan steered his car in and parked next to her.

Maxine was sitting on the couch when Dan walked through the front door. She looked from the TV to him. He knew what she was thinking.

"Not one drink," Dan said.

Maxine smiled. "I'm so proud of you."

"Oh, I wanted one."

"I bet you did."

Dan walked over to the case board and picked up the blue marker from the tray. He removed the cap and stared at the board for a second, and then under Rubino's photograph he wrote the word *gay*. He replaced the cap and laid the marker back in the tray.

"Big break in the case?" Maxine asked.

"Franco Rubino is gay."

"I see that," Maxine responded, looking at the case board.

"So it's a pretty good guess that they weren't having an affair."

"Well, that was ten years ago."

Dan turned to Maxine. "What do you mean?"

"Maybe they did have an affair. Maybe he hadn't come out yet."

"Crap." Dan grabbed the marker and put a question mark after *gay*. He folded his arms across his chest and stared at the board some more. "I really need to talk to my new friend Dave Maday some more. I hope he calls me."

"Why don't you just call him?"

"I don't want to seem pushy or needy."

"Yeah, guys hate that," said Maxine. "You should have accidentally-on-purpose left something at his house, and then called him to see if he found it."

Dan looked over to see Maxine grinning. "Like what, my bra or an earring? Smartass."

Maxine chuckled.

Dan continued looking over the board. "Maybe I'll call him on Saturday," he mumbled to himself.

Suddenly there was a loud crash and a bright flash of light. Dan jumped and Maxine screamed.

"What the Christ!" Dan shouted. He ran to the front window and looked outside. The front steps were engulfed in flames. "Call the fire department!"

Maxine leapt from the couch to get her cell phone as Dan ran toward the bedroom. He grabbed the blanket off the bed and ran for the front door.

Dan tossed the blanket over the fire and began stomping out the flames. He looked up the street one way and down the other as he stomped. He reached down and picked up a corner of the blanket and moved it over onto some smaller flames and patted them with his hands.

"Watch it!" Maxine shouted, and began pouring a gallon jug of water over the flames.

Dan moved the wet blanket around getting the last of the flames.

Maxine ran back inside for more water. When she returned the fire was out. She dumped the water over the steps any way.

"I think we got it," Dan said.

Maxine breathed a sigh of relief. "Still think store-bought water is a stupid idea?" she asked.

Dan grinned. "From now on, you buy all the bottled water you want." He picked up the soaked blanket and tossed it into the yard. He turned around and looked down at the broken bottle at his feet. There was a strong odor of gasoline.

"Who would do this?" Maxine asked.

"Who do you think?" said Dan. "Papi Garcia,"

"Oh my God."

Dan and Maxine could hear the sirens of the fire trucks off in the distance.

"Are you two okay?" Edna McGee hollered from her front porch.

"We're fine, Edna," Dan called out. He surveyed the street to see several of his neighbors on their porches and in their front yards. All were craning their necks to get a good look at the show.

"It was a black car," Old Man Stein shouted from his front yard. "Or dark blue, maybe."

"Thanks, Mr. Stein," Maxine yelled back. She gave him a little wave.

Buddy rounded the corner and plopped down in the driveway.

"Thanks for your help," Dan said to the dog.

The fire trucks rounded the corner and came to a stop in front of the house. "Where's the fire?" one of the firefighters asked as he jumped from the truck.

Dan pointed at the steps. "It was right there, but I think we got it."

The firefighter removed his glove and laid his bare hand on the top step. "Pretty warm," he commented. He put his glove back on and pulled the wooden steps away from the porch. "Spray up under here," he said, directing one of the other men.

"I think it's fine," Dan remarked.

"Better to be safe than sorry," replied the firefighter. "Wouldn't want it to rekindle."

Dan stared at the old bungalow. His eyes went from the old rusted screen that enclosed the porch to the two broken shutters attached to the attic window. "Yeah, we wouldn't want that."

Chapter Twenty-Six

Rick Carver sat behind his desk with his feet up. A half-eaten Egg McMuffin lay on its wrinkled wrapper to his right; a cup of black coffee sat next to it. "Molotov cocktail," he said. "That's original."

Dan Coast was sitting in one of the two wooden chairs in front of Rick's desk. His legs were stretched out in front of him and his fingers were interlocked behind his head. He said nothing as he stared at Rick's breakfast sandwich. His only thoughts were of making the mistake of not stopping somewhere for breakfast on his way to the police station.

"Who do you think did it?" Rick asked.

"I know who did it," Dan sneered. "It was Garcia."

"You don't *know* it was Papi Garcia."

"My neighbor saw the car."

Rick chuckled as he leaned forward to pick up his sandwich. "You mean Old Man Stein? He's a hundred years old, and according to the report I was issued this morning, he wasn't wearing his glasses, it was dark out, and he said the car was black or possibly dark blue. Garcia's car is gray."

"Close enough," Dan replied.

"Not close enough for me."

"How about fingerprints?" Dan asked.

"Fingerprints?" Rick took a big bite of his breakfast sandwich and spoke with his mouth full. "You want me to pull fingerprints from a broken bottle that you stomped on while it was on fire?" He chugged down half of his coffee and then leaned forward to grab the phone on his desk. "Here, let me call Horatio Caine, up at *CSI: Miami* or one of your other favorite cop shows and see if they can give us a hand with that."

Dan put up his hand. "Okay, okay," he said. "You don't have to be a dickhead about it."

Rick leaned back in his chair. "Well, you seem to bring out the dickhead in people."

"Are ya gonna at least talk to him?"

"No."

"Great."

"How are you coming with that other thing I gave you?" Rick asked, referring to the Maday case.

"I think we're onto something," Dan replied. "A few things are falling into place."

Rick's eyebrows rose. "Oh, really? What kind of things?"

"I'd rather not say just yet."

"You wouldn't, would ya?"

"No, and are you sure you gave me everything you had on that case?" Dan asked, knowing Rick probably hadn't.

Rick looked to the ceiling and pretended to think about it. "Yeah," he replied. "I think that was all of it."

"It's just that a lot of stuff seems to be missing from the folder."

"Like what?"

"Witness interviews, suspect list, photographs, a bunch of things."

"It's been a long time," Rick pointed out. "Things get misplaced, and sometimes things get put in the wrong folders."

"Can I look through other folders?"

"No."

"How about your computer? There must be files on the computer. Can I look on that?"

"No. I can't have you going through things like that. You get what you got. If you can solve it, good, if not, we'll shelf it."

"How about Franco Rubino, the boyfriend. Was he ever a suspect?"

"We looked at him. He had an alibi."

"What was his alibi?"

"Who knows? Ain't it in the file?"

"No."

"Sorry," Rick said. "Now, if we're all done here, I got a lot of work to do."

Dan stood. "And you're not doing anything about Garcia fire-bombing my house?"

"Not unless you bring me some hard evidence."

Dan was shaking his head on the way out of Rick's office. "Thanks for all your help," he grumbled.

"Anytime," Rick replied with a snicker.

Dan walked across the squad room, past the front desk, and out the door.

Red was sitting in the passenger seat of Dan's Porsche; the top was down as usual. "What the hell?" Red shouted. "It's friggin' hot out here. You said it would only take a second." Red rubbed his palm across his sweaty forehead and showed it to his pal.

Dan laughed. "I forgot you were even out here," he responded.

"If I was your dog I would have been dead by now."

"I doubt that." Dan opened the door and climbed into the car.

"Why, because the top is down?"

"No, because I wouldn't have left my dog in the car."

"Oh, thanks. You'll leave me sitting out here half the day, but not your dog."

Dan started the car, put it in gear, and headed out of the parking lot. "It wasn't half the day. It was a few minutes—fifteen, tops."

"Whatever," Red bitched, as he tuned the radio to a song he would enjoy. "What now?"

"Breakfast," said Dan. "Rick was eating an Egg McMuffin in there and my stomach was growling the whole time."

"So then McDonald's?"

"Christ no. I hate McDonald's."

"I thought you wanted an Egg McMuffin."

"I would imagine every restaurant in town can put an egg, a slice of cheese, and a piece of ham on an English muffin, and it will probably be a *real* egg, a *real* slice of cheese, and a *real* piece of ham."

"It's not ham, smartass," Red corrected. "It's Canadian bacon."

"Canadian bacon *is* ham."

"It is not," Red argued. "It's bacon. If it was ham they'd call it ham, ya moron."

Dan took a left onto Caroline Street. "Yeah, I'm the moron."

"Are ya gonna get it on an English muffin?"

"Probably."

"Oh, are ya, because that's not really a muffin, now is it?" Red asked with a sarcastic grin. "It's some kind of a biscuit, or something."

Dan pulled to the curb in front of Pepe's and shut off the engine. He turned to his friend. "Ya got me there, Einstein."

"Damn right I did," Red said proudly as he exited the car. "I think I'm in the mood for some French toast."

"It's not really toast, ya know?" said Dan. "It's fried bread."

"Oh shut up."

Chapter Twenty-Seven

Dan dropped Red off at the bar and grill after breakfast and went home to his empty house. Maxine was at work. Buddy was off doing whatever it is ungrateful dogs do in the afternoon, and Dan was sitting in his backyard in one of the Adirondack chairs near the fire pit. He was flipping through the morning's newspaper and sipping a warmed up cup of coffee. He closed the paper after skimming the last page, folded it, and dropped it into the dirt next to his cell phone. He stretched his legs out in front of him and dropped his head back and stared up at the slowly moving clouds above him. *Huh*, he thought. *That one looks like a big duck.* He turned his head slightly and noticed that another cloud looked like a sailboat. *Christ, not drinking is boring. How do people do this day after day?* He shut his eyes and wondered if he should fall asleep where he was, or get up and walk over to the hammock.

Dan pulled out his cell phone and dialed Dave Maday's number.

"Hello?" said Maday

"Hey, Dave. It's Dan Coast."

"Oh, hey, Dan. How's it going?"

"Not that good, Dave. Our talk the other day brought up some things, and I was wondering if you wanted to get together."

"Sure, I guess. You want to meet me for a drink at Willie T's?"

"How about Red's Bar and Grill?" Dan said. "It's usually pretty quiet this time of day."

"Sounds good," Dave agreed. "See ya there."

Dan hung up his phone and dialed Red.

"What now?" Red answered.

"Hey, I'm coming to the bar in about an hour."

"Jumping back on the wagon?" Red asked.

"It's falling off the wagon, and no, I'm not."

"So if you're off the booze, you're on the wagon?"

"Yes, now be quiet for a second," Dan scolded. "Dave Maday is coming with me."

"The guy whose wife disappeared?"

"No, the other Dave Maday, ya jack ass," Dan shot back. "Of course that Dave Maday."

"So, what do you want me to do?"

"Nothing."

"Then why did you call me?"

"Because I didn't want you to look surprised when we walked through the door. I want you to just act normal … well, as normal as you can."

"Should I call Skip?"

"Christ no! Don't do anything. Just act normal."

"You got it. But, how did this happen. Why is he gonna be with you?"

"I'll fill you in later."

"You always say you're gonna fill me in later, but that never happens."

"Well yeah, I usually just say it to shut you up." Dan hung up his cell, picked up his newspaper, and went to the house. On his way to the back door he glanced over to see Buddy lying on Bev's deck, in the sun. He thought about waving, but he knew Buddy never waved back.

Dan set his coffee mug in the sink and tossed the paper on the counter top. He went to the bathroom, took a quick shower, and changed. He walked out the front door and down the steps just as a gray Mercedes rolled slowly by.

The driver's side window of the Mercedes was down and Papi Garcia's bandaged arm hung limp over the door. He slapped the car door twice with his hand and then pointed at Dan with a big grin on his face. Even at that distance Dan could see Papi's gold front tooth gleam in the sunlight. Dan didn't smile back.

"Keep driving by, asshole!" Dan shouted.

Before he sped off, Papi's smile widened like the Grinch getting a wonderfully, awful idea.

"Oh, shit," Dan muttered. "There's gonna be trouble in Whoville."

Chapter Twenty-Eight

Dan arrived at Red's a little early, hoping he would get there before Maday.

Red looked past Dan as he entered the bar and grill. "Where is he?" Red asked.

"Shh!" replied Dan.

"I thought you said he was coming with you."

Dan climbed aboard his favorite orange bar stool. "He'll be here in a minute. I wanted to get here before him."

"So we could come up with a plan?" Red asked.

Dan rolled his eyes. "There's no plan. Christ."

"What'll ya have?"

"Ya got a root beer?"

"Not in the fountain, but I have IBC in bottles."

"So, you probably charge more for it."

"Well, yeah. It costs me more, so it costs you more."

"Bait and switch."

"Bait and switch?" Red argued. "You asked for the damn root beer. I didn't—"

"Just give me the root beer."

"Comin' right up," Red said with a smile. "That'll be two and a quarter."

"Put it on my tab."

Jocko came through the kitchen door carrying a stack of folded bar towels. He looked at Dan and then scanned the dining room. "I thought you were coming here *with* somebody," Jocko said.

"Jesus Christ," Dan said angrily. "How the hell did *he* know?"

"I thought it was best to let him in on the plan," Red said. "So he wouldn't expect anything."

"What the hell would he have expected? And for the last time, there *is* no plan. I think you've spent way too much time around Mel, because you're starting to act just like him."

Red slid Dan's root beer in front of him. "Just trying to help."

"When I want your help, I'll ask."

The front door opened and Dan turned to see Dave Maday walking into the bar. Dave nodded, and Dan nodded back. As Dave crossed the dining room floor he looked around the room. His eyes went from the two surfboards suspended from the ceiling to the neon beer signs that hung on the wall to his right. He glanced over at the old Wurlitzer that was belting out "Equal Rights" by Peter Tosh. Maday was taking in the whole place. It was obvious he had never been in Red's before … or hadn't in a long time.

Dan stood and shook hands with Maday. "What"ll ya have?" Dan asked.

Maday looked past Red and scanned the back bar. "Um … how about a shot of that American Honey over ice?"

"Comin' right up," Red said.

"You know what?" said Maday. "Make that a double."

"You got it, pal," said Red.

Maday reached for his wallet. "What are you having there, Dan?" he asked.

"I'm just having a root beer today, Dave," Dan replied. "And put your money away. This is on me."

"Well, thank you." Maday took a seat next to Dan, and looked down at Dan's half-empty bottle. "Not a drinker?"

Dan picked up the bottle and took a sip. "Oh, I'm a drinker, all right. Just been letting the old liver regenerate over the past week or so."

"How's the ankle?"

"Ankle?" Dan asked.

"The ankle you twisted in front of my house."

"Oh, yeah, the ankle. It's still a little tender. It'll be fine."

Red set Maday's drink in front of him. "There ya go." He held out his hand. "Red Baxter. Don't think I've seen you in here before."

Dave shook Red's hand. "Dave Maday. I was in here a few times about fifteen years ago."

"Before my time," Red said.

"You hungry?" Dan asked.

"Ya know, I could go for a sandwich, or something," Maday responded.

"How about we grab a table and have a look at a menu?" Dan suggested.

"Sounds good." Maday picked up his glass and followed Dan to one of the four-tops near the jukebox. Dan limped a little for effect. Seconds later, Red placed a menu in front of each man.

"Just holler when you're ready to order," Red said, and headed back to the bar.

Dan picked up his root beer, took another sip, and thought about how much it didn't taste like tequila. He sighed a little. "So, how's everything going?" he asked.

Maday slowly spun his glass with his fingertips. "Good … I guess," he replied. "Talking to you the other day did get me thinking about Elizabeth. Didn't sleep very well last night either."

"Sorry. I guess I shouldn't have asked so many questions."

Dave smiled. "No, that's fine. It was nice to talk about her with someone. Most times people won't even mention her name around me. They think they'll upset me or something. After ten years there's still not an hour of the day that some thought of her doesn't creep into my head."

"I know just what you mean," said Dan. "When you're around other people, it's like she never existed. No one talks about her. One of the things that bothers me is that I moved down here after Alex passed away, so no one down here ever even knew her."

Maday opened his menu and skimmed over both pages. Dan did the same.

"I think I'll have the BLT," said Maday.

Dan closed his menu and glanced over toward the bar. Red grabbed a pad of guest checks and returned to the table.

"All set?" Red asked, pen in hand.

"I'm going to try the BLT," Maday said.

Red looked at Dan. "Fish sandwich?"

"How'd ya guess?" Dan asked. He picked up both menus and handed them to Red.

"You said your wife passed away before you moved here," said Maday. "Where was it you came from?"

"Upstate New York," Dan replied. "Near Syracuse."

"So, your wife is buried there?"

"Yes."

"Is that hard?"

"Sometimes. But then again, sometimes I feel it's better this way."

Maday cocked his head. "Why's that?"

"Because if she were buried here, I have a feeling that I would wake up from some bad drunks lying in the cemetery and wondering how I got there."

Maday smiled. "That would be a problem."

It was Dan's turn to question. "You said they never recovered your wife's body," he began. "So there's no headstone."

"There is," Maday replied. "After so many years went by, and there was no concrete proof she was dead—and no body, the court issued a declaration of death *in absentia*. We had a small funeral. There's an empty grave in the Key

West Cemetery." Maday was quiet for a few seconds and then said, "But I've never woken up there."

Dan chuckled. "Well, good for you."

Red returned and served their orders. "Refill on those drinks?" he asked.

"That would be great," said Maday.

Both men slid their empties to the edge of the table.

"I'll have my root beer in a frosty mug this time," said Dan.

"Ain't got no frosty mugs. It'll have to be a room temperature mug."

"That'll do," said Dan. "As long as it's clean for a change."

Red picked up the empties and walked to the bar.

"Were there any suspects in her disappearance?" Dan asked Maday.

"Me, of course. And she had a coworker who they hassled for a while. There was mention that my wife was having an affair with this man, but it wasn't true. They were just really good friends. As a matter of fact, a few years later the young man came out."

"Came out of what?" Dan asked, feigning ignorance.

"The closet," Maday replied. "He was gay."

"So they probably weren't having an affair."

"Correct. He was a nice kid. I still see him places, now and then. We'll say hi, talk for a minute. Sometimes the subject will turn to Elizabeth … I guess it's because she is the only thing we have in common."

"Did he paint that portrait of Elizabeth that hangs over your fireplace?"

"No, no. That was actually painted by a coworker of *mine*," said Maday.

"After she disappeared?"

"No. About a year before."

"Was the painting done for a special occasion?"

"He painted it for Elizabeth's birthday."

"Were the two of them good friends?"

"Not really. They only knew each other through me."

"Was *he* a suspect?"

"Jake? No. He had moved away from the area at least six months before Elizabeth disappeared."

"Was he ever questioned?"

Maday looked around the room and then back at Dan. "I feel like I'm being interrogated by the police again," he said.

Dan laughed nervously. "Sorry about that. I think I just watched too many detective shows when I was growing up."

"Yeah, I understand. It's the kind of story you only see on the Lifetime channel."

"Only they wrap that up in two hours."

Dan and Maday ate their lunches, drank their drinks, and talked for another hour or so. Dan managed to slip in a few more questions. He asked if Elizabeth had worked the day she disappeared. Maday said she hadn't, that she had taken the day off. He asked if Elizabeth had acted strangely in the days leading up to her disappearance. Maday said she hadn't. He asked why Jake—Maday's coworker—had left his job, and where he had moved to. Maday seemed to recollect that Jake McKinley moved for financial reasons, and that he had moved up to North Carolina somewhere.

Dan was pleased that his questioning hadn't further aroused Maday's suspicions. The man seemed blissfully unaware of Dan's amateur sleuthing exploits, which were fast becoming part of Key West's folklore. That was to Dan's advantage.

The two men said their goodbyes, and Maday walked out the door with a head nod to Red.

Dan walked over to the bar with his empty mug and sat back down on his stool. "One more for the road," he said. "Ginger ale on ice this time. I've had my fill of root beer."

"Find out anything useful?" Red asked.

"Maybe," Dan replied. "There's a portrait some guy painted of Maday's wife. It's hanging over his fireplace."

"What's so weird about that?" Red asked, fixing Dan's drink.

"The guy who painted it was just some coworker of Maday's. He painted it for Elizabeth for her birthday. Maday said the guy and Elizabeth weren't friends, just acquaintances."

"Yeah, that sounds a little odd," Red agreed.

"The guy—Jake McKinley—left town a few months before Elizabeth disappeared, so he was never a suspect or even questioned by the police, according to Maday."

"Sounds fishy to me."

"She was wearing next to nothing in the painting. How did he know what she looked like in only a men's dress shirt? I don't know … just seems strange."

"Well, and you can trust me on this one, sexy pictures don't necessarily mean somebody's a murderer."

"And how would you know that?"

"After my divorce, I found several nude Polaroids of my wife, that I hadn't taken. They were in a shoebox on a shelf in the closet. Some guy took a lot of photographs, but sadly, the bastard didn't kill her."

"All these years and you still sound bitter," Dan chuckled.

"Yeah, well, it's a little rough to walk in on your wife when she's bent over a case of Miller Lite and the beer delivery guy is sending a package to Beaverville."

Dan laughed out loud. "I bet you still see that image when you close your eyes."

"You have no idea, my friend, no idea at all," Red admitted. "That was one hairy ass."

Chapter Twenty-Nine

Dan drove past Anna Tinka's house on his way home from Red's. He had driven by the house often in the past couple of weeks, just to check on things. Nothing ever seemed out of the ordinary, but what was *out of the ordinary*? Dan didn't know, he just felt better driving by. He wondered if Anna or Sarah ever saw him drive by, or maybe one of the neighbors. There was never anyone around. It was a quiet street. Dan thought it funny that he was driving by Anna's house, and Papi was driving past his house. Papi wasn't checking to make sure everything was fine, however, he was checking to see how he could make things not fine.

Dan looked at the car in the driveway. His eyes went to the door as well as each window, and then he sped off. He knew he would eventually have to confront Papi; he just didn't know when.

Reaching into the side pocket of his cargo shorts, Dan pulled out his cell phone, and dialed Rick Carver's number.

"What's up?" Rick answered.

"Does the name Jake McKinley ring a bell with you?" Dan asked.

There was silence for a second and then Rick replied, "No. Should it?"

"He was a coworker of Dave Maday's"

"And?"

"He painted a picture of Elizabeth Maday and gave it to her as a gift."

"Sounds like a nice guy."

"So if someone you worked with painted a half-naked picture of Laura and gave it to her as a birthday gift, the first thing you would think is, *nice guy*?"

"What half was naked?" Rick inquired.

"She was only wearing a men's dress shirt, unbuttoned to show plenty of boobage."

"Sounds a little odd," Rick agreed. "But we don't really know what their relationship was or how close they were. Did it seem like it bothered Maday?"

"Not in the least."

"Well, there ya go. Probably harmless."

"Maybe. Or maybe it doesn't bother him now, but it bothered him then."

"Did we question him?" Rick asked.

"No. Maday said that McKinley moved away about six months before Laura went missing."

"Then the detective probably didn't see any need to speak with him."

"Myron Danks is listed as lead detective in the case file. Good cop?" Dan asked. He pulled into his driveway and shut off the engine.

"Of course he was a good cop."

"*Was*?"

"He's no longer with the department."

"Retired?"

"Dead. Heart attack last year."

"So speaking with him is out of the question."

"Unless you have a Ouija board."

"Can you at least look up Jake McKinley for me? Maday said he moved up to North Carolina somewhere."

"I can do that," Rick replied unenthusiastically.

"Also, Papi Garcia keeps driving by my house."

"It's not a crime to drive down your street."

"He's trying to intimidate me."

"Is it working?"

"No."

"Then don't worry about it."

"I'm worried about Maxine."

"Why? *Her* dog didn't bite him?"

Chapter Thirty

It was six o'clock in the evening as Dan Coast stood in his living room staring at the case board. He had printed out the photograph he had taken of Elizabeth Maday's portrait. The photo was stuck to the board next to a blue stick figure Dan had drawn. Underneath the stick figure was the name Jake McKinley.

Dan heard the screen door creak behind him, and turned to see Rick Carver walking onto his front porch; he carried a file folder with him. Dan waved him in.

"What the hell is that monstrosity?" Rick asked as he walked through the front door.

"That's my case board," Dan replied proudly.

Rick stepped closer and scanned the photographs and notes scattered about the board. "I thought I told you not to take pictures of the files," he said.

"You did."

"But of course, you didn't listen."

"That's on you for trusting me. You should have known better. Also, I would have hidden the board if you hadda called and said you were coming over."

Rick pulled a sheet of paper from the file folder. "Here."

"What's this?" Dan asked, taking it.

"The information about Jake McKinley you asked for. That's him in the photograph."

"That was easy," he said, and began reading.

Rick went ahead and told Dan what was on the paper. "Jake McKinley lives in North Carolina with Carrie, his wife of nine years, in a little town called Manns Harbor."

"Wife of nine years, huh," Dan replied. "I wonder if she's a tall red head that looks fantastic wearing nothing but a men's dress shirt." Dan stuck the paper Rick had given him to the case board with one of the magnets that lay in the tray below it. "Elizabeth could have changed her name to Carrie."

Rick grinned. "That was the first thing I checked." He opened the folder again. Inside was another paper, with a photograph of a woman in her early forties—a brunette. "Carrie's maiden name was Compo. She's forty-three years old. She's never changed her name, other than when she got married."

"Maybe Carrie Compo was the name Elizabeth Maday stole from someone else. Maybe Carrie Compo was a real person at one time," Dan suggested. "Maybe she died and then Elizabeth used her name so there would be a record of her. Maybe they got her name off a head stone in a cemetery or something." Dan took the paper and inspected the photo. "It's been ten years. This could be her."

Rick guffawed at Dan's overactive imagination. "If I've said it once, Coast, I've said it a hundred times: you watch way too much television. Stealing a dead person's identity and obtaining a birth certificate and driver's license, and whatever else you would need to make it look legit, isn't as easy as it looks on TV."

"But it could be done?"

"Yeah, it could be, but—"

"So you'll look into it?"

"No. I won't."

Dan turned back to McKinley's information. "It says here that McKinley was arrested twice in the past."

"Yeah, once when he was eighteen, and again when he was twenty; both times for shoplifting. He's had a clean record for the last twenty-five years."

"Or maybe he just hasn't been caught."

Rick gave Dan a condescending chuckle as he retrieved his gold-rimmed aviators from his shirt pocket and slid them on. "I gotta go, Laura's probably got supper on the table."

Dan folded the paper and stuck it in his front pocket. "Did you call McKinley's old boss at Southern Most Pool and Spa to see why he left?"

"Yes. The boss—Lane Crone—said as far as he could remember, Jake McKinley was a model employee. He gave a two-week notice, and moved away."

"What do you mean, *as far as he could remember*?"

"Just that. From what Crone remembered, McKinley was a good employee. It was ten years ago."

"Which was he," Dan asked. "Good, or model?"

"I don't know. He said he wasn't actually the boss back then, his dad was."

"Maybe the dad has something else to say about McKinley."

"I gave Crone your phone number and told him to call you if he remembered anything, or if his dad thought of anything." Rick turned and headed toward the door. "I gotta go."

"I'm gonna solve this," Dan said.

"I'm looking forward to it, Barnaby Jones."

Maxine met Rick on the front porch. "You here to arrest him?" she asked with a hopeful smile.

"Not this time, Maxine," Rick replied. "How are you today?"

"Good, Rick. You?"

"Great, now," Rick said. "That boyfriend of yours sure cheers me up with all his foolishness."

"You should live with him. It's a laugh a minute."

"I bet it is, I bet it is." Rick went on down the steps and to his car.

"Honey, I'm home," Maxine announced. She walked over and gave Dan a peck on the cheek. "What's for dinner?"

"Whatever you feel like making," Dan replied.

"I worked all day."

Dan pointed at the case board. "So did I!"

Maxine kicked off her Crocs, and using her big toes slid off each sock. "Any breakthroughs in the big case?"

Dan was scratching his chin as he stared at the clues. "You don't have to say it like that."

"Like what?"

"*Big case.*"

"What's wrong with big case?"

"It sounds like you're making fun of me," Dan complained. "I don't refer to your job as your *big nursing job.*"

Maxine put her arms around her man. "I wouldn't make fun of a *big* private investigator like you."

"Why do I even talk?"

"I have no idea," Maxine replied. "I'm going to change and then you can take me out to dinner."

"Okay. Do you have tomorrow off?"

"Yes."

"I'll probably be gone most of the day."

"Where are you going?"

"I'm gonna see if Phil will fly me and Red up to Manns Harbor. There's a guy up there that used to work with Dave Maday and I need to talk with him."

Maxine pointed at the photograph Dan had taken of the painting of Elizabeth. "Is that her?"

"Yes."

"She was pretty."

"She probably still is."

"You think she's still alive?"

"Yes."

"But Rick doesn't?"

"No. He thinks I watch too much television."

"No comment."

"Do you think I watch too much television?"

"You watch an awful lot of television."

Dan pointed across the room at his bottle of tequila. "I gave up the booze, Maxine. I'm not giving up TV."

"I wouldn't want you to. They say the withdrawals from TV can be fatal."

"Walk away, Maxine. Walk away."

Chapter Thirty-One

"You want me to drive?" Maxine asked.

"Why?" Dan asked, on his way to the car. "I haven't been drinking, and I won't be drinking at dinner."

"Oh, that's right. Sorry."

"Whatever." Dan climbed into his car.

"How long's it been?"

"Why does everyone keep asking me that?"

"They're proud of you."

Dan shot her a look. "Proud of me? No one is proud of me. No one gives a shit."

Maxine got in and Dan started the engine. "Well, I'm proud of you." She leaned over and kissed him on the cheek.

"Awesome." Dan backed out of the driveway and headed up the street. He took a left at the end of the street and another left onto Sky View Street.

"Where are you going?" Maxine asked.

"I was just gonna drive by the Tinkas' place."

"How many times have you done that in the past week?"

"A few," Dan admitted. "I'm an idiot."

"You're not an idiot for worrying about someone."

Anna Tinka and Sarah were walking out their front door as Dan and Maxine drove slowly by. Sarah smiled big and waved. "Maxine!" she called out.

Anna looked to her daughter and then at the Porsche. Maxine smiled and waved back. Dan pulled to the curb.

"What are you doing?' Maxine asked.

"Let's go talk to them," Dan replied. "You keep Sarah busy while I talk with her mother."

"Are you sure this is a good idea?"

"Probably not."

Anna Tinka glared at the couple as they walked toward her. Sarah ran to Maxine and threw her arms around her.

"Sarah," her mother scolded. "Get back over here!"

"Can we talk for a second?" Dan asked.

"About what?" Anna said angrily.

"About your job," Dan said.

Maxine steered Sarah away from the house as they spoke.

"What about my job?" Anna asked. "I don't suppose you're looking to hire me."

"No," Dan assured her. "I just want to talk."

Anna looked at her watch. "It's three hundred dollars for the first hour. Start talking."

"Seriously?"

"Seriously."

"I was told that you've tried to—"

"In advance," Anna said, extending her hand with the palm up.

Dan reached for his money clip and counted out two hundreds and two fifties. He laid them in Anna's hand.

"I was told that you've tried to end your business relationship with Papi Garcia in the past."

"Business relationship," Anna repeated with a snort, as she shoved the cash into the front pocket of her jean shorts. "Who told you that?"

"It doesn't matter. Is it true? Do you want out?"

"And what if I do?"

"I'll get you out."

"There's no getting out. When I get a little older and Papi can't make the money off me that he used to, he'll just let me go."

"And when will that be?"

"Who knows? Six or seven years, maybe."

"Sarah will be what, sixteen or seventeen by then? This how you want her to grow up?"

"How I raise my kid is my business."

"How you raise your kid is *everyone's* business," Dan argued. "It takes a village, like they say. Let me help you."

"Noble talk. But it doesn't matter anyway. This is what I do. You can't help me, no one can."

"If you want out, just give the word."

"What would I do after I *got out*?"

"You get a real job."

Anna looked down the street at Sarah and Maxine. "Come on, Sarah!" she shouted. "We gotta go."

Dan reached out and gently took a hold of Anna's arm. "Think about what I've said."

Anna pulled her arm away. "I'll think about it."

Sarah ran back to her mother. "See ya, Maxine," she said. "Bye, Mr. Dan!"

"Be sweet, Sarah," said Maxine. She and Anna traded cold, appraising looks, woman to woman.

Dan and Maxine returned to Dan's car and the two drove off down the street.

"Well," Maxine asked. "Did it go as you hoped?"

"She's gonna think about it."

"What's there to think about?"

Dan just shrugged his shoulders and reached for his cell and dialed.

"Island Adventures," came a voice from the other end. "Phil speaking."

"Phil, it's Dan."

"What do you want this time?" Phil grumbled.

"Ouch. What's that supposed to mean?"

"I haven't heard from you in a few months … since you wanted to borrow two jet skis."

"Oh, yeah," Dan replied. "Thanks for letting me borrow those."

"You're welcome. And now back to my original question, what do you want this time?"

"I was wondering if you could give me a ride somewhere."

"I thought you got a new car."

"In your plane."

"Where to?"

"Manns Harbor."

"North Carolina?"

"You've heard of it?"

"Of course."

"So, can you do it?"

"When?"

"Tomorrow."

"No can do."

"The next day?"

"Hold on."

Dan could hear papers being shuffled around. "What time?"

"Ten in the morning."

"Okay, but I've gotta be back here by six that evening."

"No problem," Dan assured him. "Probably have you back by three."

"Even better."

"Thanks, Phil."

"Yeah."

"Bye."

"B—"

Dan tossed his cell onto the dashboard.

Chapter Thirty-Two

Dan heard the cell phone vibrate and rolled over in bed. He looked at the clock; it was four a.m. The phone vibrated again; he reached for it. "Maxine," he said. "Maxine, it's yours."

"Wh … what?"

"Your cell phone is ringing."

Maxine grabbed the cell phone as it danced across the top of the nightstand. "Hello?" she asked groggily.

"Maxine?" came a little voice from the earpiece.

"Who is this?"

"It's Sarah."

Maxine sat up and nudged Dan. "What's the matter, Sarah? Are you okay?"

"Mr. Garcia is here. He's really angry, and he's yelling at my mom. I'm scared."

Maxine nudged Dan again, this time with her knee.

"What?" Dan mumbled.

"It's Sarah," Maxine said. "Sarah, where is your mom?"

"They're in her bedroom," Sarah replied.

Dan grabbed the phone from Maxine. "Sarah, it's Dan. Are you hurt?"

"No. Mr. Garcia is really drunk, and he keeps yelling."

"Sarah, I want you to be as quiet as you can and go get in your closet and shut the door."

"I don't have a closet."

"Can you get under your bed?"

"Yes."

"Then do it, and stay on the phone. Don't get out from under your bed, no matter what, until I get there."

"Okay."

"I'm gonna give the phone back to Maxine."

"Okay. Please hurry. I'm worried about my mom."

"I'll be right there."

Dan handed the phone back to Maxine and then grabbed his own phone. "Here, call 911, then call Rick. His number is in my contacts. Tell him what's going on."

Dan jumped over Maxine to the floor and pulled open the nightstand drawer. He reached inside and grabbed his 9mm. He flipped on the bedroom light and quickly pulled on his shorts as Maxine dialed for help.

"Be careful," Maxine said as Dan headed for the door. He didn't answer.

Dan ran through the front door, locking it and pulling it closed behind him. He ran across the street and through

Edna McGee's yard with his pistol in one hand and his T-shirt in the other. He was barefoot and running as fast as he could. He clumsily put on his T-shirt as he ran.

When he got to Sky View Street he slowed, and surveyed his surroundings. Anna's car was in the driveway, and parked behind it was Papi Garcia's Mercedes. A light glowed in the front window. The porch light was off. Dan gripped his weapon tightly as he made his way up the walk and onto the porch. He stopped at the door and listened. There were no sounds coming from inside. He reached down and gently turned the doorknob; it was unlocked. He pushed the door open but stayed on the porch. Still he heard nothing.

Dan stepped quietly into the house. He could now see Anna in the kitchen. She was standing at the sink wetting a dish towel and wiping her face. Dan moved quietly toward her.

Anna turned her head just as Dan got to her. She started to speak, but Dan put his hand over her mouth.

"Where is he?" Dan whispered.

Anna pulled his hand away. "He left. What are you doing here?"

Anna's lip was swollen and bloody. There was a welt over one of her eyes that was turning purple as they spoke. Mascara trailed down her cheeks.

"Sarah called and said you were in trouble," Dan said.

"And you came to rescue us," Anna wiped her face with the dish towel. "Well, you're too late, he's gone. Now, why don't you get the hell out of my house, my big hero?"

Dan ignored Anna's sarcasm and instead went in search of Sarah. Anna followed him down the hallway.

"Sarah!" Dan called out.

"Mr. Dan!" Sarah shouted back.

Dan opened the bedroom door to see Sarah crawling out from under her bed. He slipped his gun into the back of his waistband. She ran to him and hugged him.

Dan took the phone from her. "Everything is fine, Maxine," he said into the phone.

"She hung up when I told her you were here," said Sarah.

Dan tossed the phone onto Sarah's bed.

"See, Mom," Sarah said. "He came to help us just like he said he would."

"Yeah, that's great," Anna said. "He gets us into trouble and then comes to our rescue." She turned to Dan. "If you would have just left us alone, this wouldn't have happened."

"What do you mean?" Dan asked.

"Sarah told Papi you were here today. She told him I might be getting a *new job*," Anna explained. "That was the *last* thing Papi wanted to hear."

Dan could hear sirens in the distance. "Where did he go?" he asked. "His car is still in the driveway."

"How the hell would I know? He's been smoking all day. He's not in his right mind."

"Smoking what?"

"Crank. He gets crazy when he does that shit."

"Think. Where would he go?"

Anna chuckled. "I kinda thought he might pay you a little visit."

Dan's eyes widened. "What do you mean? What did he say?"

"He said something about you trying to take his best girl, and that maybe he'd show you how that felt."

Dan reached for his weapon and ran to the door. As he got to the porch, two Key West patrol cars, with lights flashing and sirens blaring, lurched to a stop in front of the house. Officers leapt from both cars with their guns drawn.

"Drop the weapon!" one of the officers shouted. His gun was pointing at Dan.

"Drop it!" another shouted. Dan froze.

"He's at my house!" Dan shouted.

"Drop the gun!"

Dan did as he was told.

"Get on the ground!"

"Gacia is at my house!" Dan shouted.

Two of the officers ran toward him, never taking their weapons off him.

"On the ground!"

The lead officer grabbed the front of Dan's shirt. Dan pulled away. The other cop hit Dan in the chest with his shoulder. Dan reeled backward against the house. Pinned and outnumbered, Dan threw wild punches as the officers struggled to cuff him, cussing a blue streak all the while.

Rick Carver's Ford Bronco pulled up.

"Rick!" Dan shouted.

"Relax!" said one of the cops. "Stop fighting us."

When Rick got to the porch he grabbed the shoulder of one of the officers. "Carl, stop!" he said.

"He had a gun," Carl replied.

"Let him up," said Rick.

The two cops backed off and Dan got to his knees. Rick helped him to his feet. Blood was coming from Dan's nose and a small cut on his forehead.

Dan wiped the blood away from his top lip with the back of his hand. "Rick … Garcia is … at my house," he panted.

"Jesus Christ! Come on."

Dan grabbed his 9mm off the porch floor. He and Rick ran across the street in the direction of Dan's house.

"Six three two Beach View Street!" Rick shouted over his shoulder as he ran.

The four cops jumped back in their cruisers.

Dan was to the house first; he ran up the front steps and onto the porch.

Rick was a few feet behind Dan, and ran down the driveway.

Dan peeked through the glass panel of the front door, turned the knob, and shoved open the door. Just as he entered the living room, Papi Garcia exited the hallway into the dining room. He had his left arm around Maxine's throat. The .38 revolver in his right hand was pressed to her temple. Maxine's face was a horrible shade of red and her eyes were popping and bloodshot. The tip of her tongue protruded through her bluish lips. Her pajamas, top and bottom, were askew, whether from struggling or Papi's pawing Dan didn't know, and he didn't like to guess.

Dan's blood boiled. He felt his pulse jackhammering in his chest as he pointed his 9mm at Papi's head.

"Drop the gun, smart-ass," said Papi calmly. His speech was slurred, and he spat as he spoke. His eyes were wide and wild.

Dan kept the gun trained. "I'm not gonna do that," he said.

"Drop it or I'll put a tunnel through this bitch's head."

The back door swung open and Rick stepped into the kitchen; his gun was also aimed at Papi. Papi turned sideways to keep the two men in his sight.

"Put down your weapon and move away from her," Rick ordered.

A scary grin came over Papi's face. "I'm going to count to three and if you two don't lay down—"

Rick pulled his trigger and the side of Papi's head exploded.

Time stood still for a fraction of a second, and then Garcia dropped straight to the floor, still gripping his pistol.

Maxine stumbled forward, catching herself with the palms of her hands on the edge of the dining room table.

Dan ran to Maxine and Rick ran to Garcia, kicking his .38 across the room.

Dan put his arms around Maxine; she was shaking uncontrollably. Her face, hair, and torso were splattered with gore and chunks of Garcia's skull and brains. "Everything is okay," he said. "You're okay."

Rick looked Maxine over. "Are you hurt?" His voice was soft and apologetic. "I had to take the shot. I had no choice …" his voice trailed off.

Maxine said nothing but only stared into Dan's face as if she didn't recognize him.

Chapter Thirty-Three

Maxine sat at the end of the sofa with a blanket around her shoulders. An old episode of *The Rifleman* played on AMC, but Maxine was so far away in her thoughts that the television might as well have been off. She stared straight through the TV as the early morning's traumatic events ran in an endless loop through her mind.

"Can I get you anything?" Dan asked, his girlfriend.

Maxine shook her head no. Her eyes were still red and swollen from crying. She still looked just as scared as she did six hours earlier.

"I can make you some breakfast," Dan offered.

She shook her head no again.

"I'm sorry," Dan said.

There was no reply.

Dan looked over at Buddy, who lay on his flannel bed, and then back at Maxine. "I'm gonna drive over to

Dave Maday's," he said. "Are you gonna be alright here by yourself?"

She nodded yes, and then lay back with her head on the armrest. She pulled the blanket tighter around her shoulders.

Dan turned and walked out the front door. When he got to the bottom of the steps he pulled out his cell and dialed Bev's number.

"Hello?"

"Bev, it's Dan."

"Hey, how is everything?"

"Not great," Dan replied. "I was wondering if you could come over and sit with Maxine while I run somewhere." Dan opened his car door and climbed in. "I shouldn't be that long."

"Sure," Bev said. "I'll be over in a few minutes."

"Thanks, Bev." Dan hung up his cell, tossed it onto the seat next to him, and backed out of the driveway. Bev was already walking out of her front door as Dan drove by. Bev smiled and waved, and Dan waved back.

Dan pulled his car to the curb in front of Dave Maday's house. When he got out of the car and walked up the walkway, he looked over his shoulder at Maday's elderly neighbor, who was once again raking his front lawn. The old man glared at Dan. Dan wondered if the old codger recognized him. He hoped not, since he was not in the mood for another foot chase.

Dan knocked on the door three times and waited about four seconds before ringing the doorbell.

"I'm coming, I'm coming," came Dave's voice from inside the house.

Dave pulled open the door. "Hey, Dan," he said with a smile. "What's up?"

"Can I come in, Dave?" Dan asked. His voice was without inflection, his expression blank.

The smile left Maday's face. "Is everything okay?" He stepped away from the door, allowing Dan to enter.

"You might better sit down for this," said Dan.

"Oooh-kay," Dave replied suspiciously. "You're starting to worry me a little." He sat down on the couch and Dan sat across from him in a chair.

"Dave … I think I found your wife."

Dave shook his head like he was just waking up from a nap. "Wait … what? My wife? What do you mean?"

Dan glanced over at the painting of Elizabeth and then back at Dave. "This might sound crazy", he warned. "But Dave McKinley—the guy who painted the picture— is living up in Manns Harbor."

"Yeah, I told you he move up to North Carolina somewhere. What does that have to do with Elizabeth?"

"McKinley was married about a year after he moved up there … to a woman who matches your wife's description."

"What do you mean, matches her description?"

Dan pulled the document Rick gave him from his front pocket and unfolded it. He leaned forward and dropped it on the coffee table. "I think this is your wife."

Maday moved in for a closer look. "It says this woman's name is Carrie McKinley."

"That's her name now," Dan said, "but I think she may have changed it. Imagine her ten years younger, with a different hair do, and red hair.

Dave stared at the picture. He moved his glasses down his nose a little and then back as he inspected it. "Yeah, maybe," he agreed. "It could be her. Do you have another photograph? This one is kind of blurry, and her hair is over her face."

"That's the only photo I have."

Maday picked up the photograph and set back in his seat. "What should I do?"

"A friend of mine can fly us up to Manns Harbor tomorrow morning at ten."

"My God," Maday said quietly. "Do you think it could really be her?"

Dan shrugged. "I admit it's a long shot. But don't you want to know for sure?"

Maday pondered the offer for a second and then said, "Let's do it. Let's go up there."

"I'll pick you up tomorrow morning at nine."

The two men got up from their seats and Maday walked Dan to the door. "I have to ask, Dan, why did you do this? What made you look into my wife's disappearance in the first place?"

Dan looked back at the painting. "I don't know. Something about your coworker painting that portrait of your wife just didn't sit right with me," he said. "The whole story sounded a little funny, so I spoke about it with a friend of mine who's a cop."

"Was he a cop back when she disappeared?" Maday asked.

"Yeah, he was a cop then, but he's the chief of police now."

"Carver," said Maday.

"Yeah, Rick Carver. Know him?"

"Just by reputation. Likes to grandstand, from what I've heard."

Dan grinned at the apt description. "Oh, Rick's all right, once you get to know him."

"Does he know we're flying up there tomorrow?"

"Christ no!" said Dan. "The less he knows, the better. I'll fill him in on everything after it's all over."

Dan turned and started out the door. Maday gave him a friendly slap on the back. "Hopefully it'll all be over soon."

Chapter Thirty-Four

Dan pulled up to the curb in front of his house, on the wrong side of the street, and facing the wrong direction. Rick Carver came to a stop in his white Bronco, right in front of Dan. Both men got out of their vehicles. Rick was dressed in his street clothes.

"You're parked the wrong way," Rick informed him.

"Luckily it's your day off," Dan replied.

"I have the next four days off," Rick said.

"Vacation, huh?"

"Not exactly. I'll be on restricted duty for a few days any way because of the shooting, so I figured it would be a good time to take a couple days off."

"What do you mean?" Dan asked.

"Fire your weapon, get investigated," Rick responded.

"You didn't do anything wrong. Besides, you're the chief of police."

"No kidding, but it's procedure. They'll probably contact you on Monday to give a statement."

"So that's why you're here," Dan grinned big and nodded his head. "You want to make sure we all get our stories straight."

Rick lowered his head and peered over the top of his aviators. "There's no story, Coast. Just tell 'em what happened."

"Hmm." Dan tapped his chin with his index finger. "It's all kind of a blur. It happened so fast."

Rick turned and started toward the front door. "You're a real asshole."

"No one's ever called me that before."

"Yeah, right."

The two men walked up the steps and into the house. Maxine was still on the couch. She was sitting up again and had a small plate on her lap that held two pieces of dry toast. There was a bite out of the corner of one piece.

Bev walked from the kitchen into the dining room. "Hey, guys," she said. She was holding a cup of coffee. She brought the cup to Maxine and set it on the end table next to her. "Here ya go, sweetheart."

"How ya doing, Maxine?" Rick asked.

"A little better," Maxine said. "My ears are still ringing."

"Yeah," Rick said. "Gunshots are pretty loud when they're indoors."

"And right next to your head," Maxine added.

"He had no choice, Maxine," Dan said.

Maxine shot Dan a ferocious look. "He shouldn't have had to make a choice. That piece of shit pimp shouldn't have been in our home to begin with."

"I know," Dan replied. "I'm sorry."

"That doesn't help," said Maxine.

Rick nodded his head toward the door, and he and Dan went back outside. "You think she's gonna be okay?" Rick asked.

"She'll be fine," Dan assured him. "She's tough."

"Okay. Let me know if you need anything." Rick stuck out his hand and they shook. When Rick got to the driver's side of the Bronco he said, "I'm thinking about going fishing in the morning. You game?"

"I don't think so," Dan replied. "I've got some shit to do tomorrow. Thanks anyway, though."

"What do you got to do that's so important?"

"I'm investigating an old murder."

Rick chuckled. "Stickin' with it, huh?"

"I know you didn't give me all the information you had on that case."

Rick was still smiling. He said nothing.

"You don't have to admit it," said Dan. "I know you were just trying to give me something to do, to get me off your back."

"I would never," Rick said, faking innocence.

"I'm gonna solve it."

"Like I said, I'm looking forward to it. Hell, I might even see if we can scrounge up another citation for ya. Maybe it won't rain this time."

Dan scratched the bridge of his nose with his middle finger, and mouthed the words *fuck you.*

Chapter Thirty-five

With Dave Maday in the passenger seat, Dan piloted the Porsche along Seaside Way until he came to the billboard that read ISLAND ADVENTURES: LAND, SEA, AIR, and pulled into the parking lot. Island Adventures was owned by Phil Lambert and his wife April, longtime friends of Dan and Red. Phil, a retired Navy man, went to work at Island Adventures soon after he and April arrived in Key West, and after a few years purchased the business from its owner, Buck Mathers.

Dan skidded to a stop next to Red's pink Volkswagen Bug. The men got out of the car and headed across the parking lot to the office. A small bell rang when Dan opened the office door.

"Mornin', Dan," said April. She sat behind an old metal desk in front of three, four-foot, metal filing cabinets.

April was petite, around five-three, and had light brown hair she wore in a bob. She was in her early fifties, but still looked an awful lot like the high school cheerleader and homecoming queen she once was.

"Morning, April," Dan replied with a smile. If anyone ever accused Dan of having a slight crush on the woman ten years his senior, he probably wouldn't dispute it. April was the all-around perfect wife as far as Dan was concerned, and Phil was one of the luckiest men on the island. "This Is Dave Maday. Dave, April."

"Nice to meet you, April," said Maday.

"Likewise." April pointed at the table against the wall behind them. "There's coffee and muffins on the table. Help yourself."

"Homemade?" Dan asked.

"Of course," April replied.

"Don't mind if I do." As Dan leaned over the table to make his selection, Maday caught glimpse of the 9mm tucked into the front of his waistband. He registered no reaction.

"No thanks," Maday said. "I ate a big breakfast this morning."

"You're not gonna want to turn down one of April's muffins," Dan argued.

Maday inspected the table. "Aw, ya talked me into it." He poured some coffee into a Styrofoam cup, added three packets of sugar, and two creamers, and picked up one of the blueberry muffins.

"They down at the plane?" Dan asked.

"You got it. They're just waiting for you latecomers."

"Latecomer? Nobody ever called me that," Dan said. "But sometimes I'm an early com—"

"Spare your locker room humor and get the hell outta here!" said April good-naturedly.

As they rounded the corner of the hangar Dan could see Red and Phil standing on the dock next to the 1966 DHC-2 Beaver, a seaplane equipped with pontoons, or floats, under the fuselage to provide buoyancy. The yellow plane looked like a relic from a bygone era but Dan wasn't worried about its safety, knowing Phil kept his stock in tip-top condition.

When they reached the dock, Red and Phil were in the middle of a heated discussion.

"Mornin', Phil," said Dan. He introduced Maday and asked, "This bastard giving you grief?"

"Mornin', Dan. Yeah, Red just called my plane an old crate. Them's fightin' words!"

"It is an old crate," Red insisted. "I think I saw it the other day on a rerun of *Flipper*. And the fact that your mechanic's been poking around the crate for the last fifteen minutes don't exactly fill me with confidence."

"Derrick was just performing a pre-flight safety inspection and found a little glitch," Phil said, trying to keep his cool. "Standard procedure."

"I bet," Red mumbled.

Derrick White climbed out of the cockpit. "I don't know what the problem was," he said. "Seems fine now."

"One of the flaps was sticking, chief," Derrick replied. "But it's all good now." Derrick called everyone chief, boss, or champ.

"Yeah," Red said. "Everything's fine till we hit the water. You know, they say hitting the water from that altitude is just like hitting concrete."

"Who are *they*?" Dan asked.

"I don't know," Red replied. "The people who study plane crashes, I guess."

"We're not gonna crash!" Phil screamed in exasperation.

"We better not," Red warned. "I got a lot to live for."

"Name one thing," Dan said.

"Why don't you name … shut up."

"Good one," Dan said to the laughter of the others.

The four men climbed aboard the vintage yellow seaplane and were off.

Chapter Thirty-Six

Arriving in Mann's Harbor later that day, Phil taxied the Beaver up to the dock at the end of Old Ferry Dock Road. Dan jumped out and tethered the plane to the dock, and Phil shut down the engines. Maday and Red climbed out and jumped from one of the pontoons to the dock.

"See, we didn't crash," Phil said.

"We still gotta get back," Red replied.

Phil jumped to the dock last. "I'll wait here with the plane," he said. "You go do what ya gotta do, and make it quick." He looked at his wristwatch. "Real quick. I've got an appointment, remember."

Dan, Red, and Maday started down the dock toward town.

"So where is this place?" Red asked.

Dan pulled the folded piece of paper with the address from his pocket. "It's 6393 Preston Twiford Road."

"Ain't there any directions on how to get there on that paper?"

"No."

A tow-headed boy of nine or ten was walking toward them. He carried a tackle box in one hand and an old Zebco rod & reel combo in the other. With his freckles, rolled up jeans, and bare feet, the kid was the picture of a modern-day Tom Sawyer.

"Hey, kid," Dan said. "We're looking for Preston Twiford Road."

The boy turned and pointed up the street. "Just go down this road here to Sixty-four, and take your first right."

"Thanks, kid," Dan said.

"How far is it?" Red asked.

"'Bout a half a mile," the kid replied. "Say, you guys lost or something?"

"Why, do we look lost?" said Dan.

The kid looked them up and down critically. "Yeah. You look like a bunch of tourists to me."

"We're not tourists, ya little smartass," said Dan defensively. "We're undercover CIA agents on a secret mission for the president."

The kid broke into a snaggletooth grin. "Bullshit! I'll see you guys later." He headed down the road.

"Kids today, huh?" Red said. He looked to Dan. "Should we call a cab?"

"A cab?" Dan responded. "The punk said it's only a half mile. We can walk it in ten minutes."

"Fine," Red groaned. "Ya know I got bad hips."

Dan stopped and pointed back down the dock. "You wanna wait in the plane?"

"No."

"Because you can wait in the plane."

"I don't want to wait in the plane."

"Then quit your bitchin'!"

The three men resumed their trek and in about ten minutes they were there.

The McKinley place was an old lime green trailer on the left side of the street. Unlike most of the other trailers on the road, the McKinleys' seemed to be well taken care of. Unlike the other lots, there were no junk cars or old appliances littering their property. A single car sat in the driveway, a red 1999 Saturn.

"This is the place," Dan said.

"What if he starts trouble?" Red asked.

Dan lifted the front of his shirt to show his pistol grip.

Maday stared at the single-wide. "I have to tell you, this doesn't look like a place my Elizabeth would live."

"We'll soon find out," said Red, and started for the trailer. Dan and Maday followed. Dan walked up the steps and onto the deck; the other two waited in the yard. Dan knocked on the door.

After a few seconds the door opened and standing in front of Dan was the man in the photograph Rick had given him. "Can I help you?" the man asked.

"Are you Jake McKinley?" Dan asked.

"What's this about?"

"We're looking for a man by the name of Jake McKinley. Are you him?" Dan held up the photograph.

"'Cause you sure look like him to me." Dan pushed by the man and went inside the trailer.

"Hey, wait. What are you doing?"

"Elizabeth!" Dan shouted.

"I'm calling the police," said McKinley.

Dan stopped and turned around to face him. "Yeah, you go ahead and call the cops, and we'll wait while you explain to them how you stole this man's wife"—Dan pointed at Maday as he entered the room—"and how you and her faked her death."

"Stole his wife?" McKinley asked. "What the hell are you talking about?"

"You're saying you never worked with Dave Maday at Southern Most Pool and Spa in Key West?"

"I never lived in Key West. You've got me mixed up with my brother, James."

Dan looked from McKinley to Maday, and then back. "What?"

"That was my brother James that lived in Key West. He was probably using my name. He's done it several times. He racked up over ten grand in credit card debt in my name once."

Dan looked back at Maday. "Is he lying?"

Maday shrugged. "I don't know. He could be telling the truth. He looks a little like I remember, but … I don't know."

"Christ!" Dan said.

Just then a blue Ford Escort pulled into the driveway. A tall brunette got out of the car and walked up to the trailer and onto the deck. Red smiled and nodded. She cautiously looked through the doorway. "What's going on?" she asked, stepping inside.

"Carrie, these gentlemen are looking for my brother," McKinley said. "They think I'm him."

"Is this your wife, Dave?" Dan asked.

Maday shook his head no. "I've never seen that woman before in my life."

"Christ!"

Red couldn't help but chuckle.

"Where's your brother now, McKinley?" Dan asked.

"I have no idea," McKinley replied. "I haven't seen him in eleven or twelve years."

Dan dropped his head and stared at the brown shag carpeting for a second. "Come on, let's go," he said. "Sorry for the intrusion."

Red was still snickering when Dan got to the front steps. "You want to try one of the other trailers?" he needled.

"Shut it," Dan replied on his way by.

Chapter Thirty-Seven

Somewhere over the Atlantic Ocean, Red and Phil were still laughing, and Dan was still sulking. Dave Maday sat quietly in the back seat next to Dan.

"I don't understand," Dan remarked. "I was so sure."

"Me either," Red agreed. "It's not like you to screw up." He and Phil burst out laughing again.

"You guys are assholes," Dan grumbled.

"Yeah," Phil jabbed. "*We're* the assholes."

"Can you turn on the radio, Red?" Dan asked. "Maybe the music will drown out the two of you."

Maday spoke up. "In Dan's defense, he was just trying to help me out. And he was right, Jake McKinley did live there."

"The *wrong* Jake McKinley," Red argued.

Dan's cell phone began ringing. "What now?" he mumbled, and pulled the cell from his pocket. He looked at the number on the screen. "Who's this?"

"Maybe it's another Jake McKinley," said Phil.

Red snorted.

"Hello?" Dan said.

"Dan Coast?" the caller asked.

"It's me," Dan replied.

"Mr. Coast, this is Lane Crone."

"Lane Crone?" Dan asked.

Maday's eyes shot to Dan.

"From Southern Most Pool," Crone said. "Chief Carver gave me your number."

"Oh, yeah," Dan said. "What can I do for you?"

"I was speaking to my father this morning about Jake McKinley. I asked him if he could remember why McKinley left."

"And?"

"He said McKinley didn't quit. My father had to let him go."

"Why did he let him go?" Dan and Maday locked eyes.

Red continued to search for a radio station.

"He said McKinley lied on his job application. When asked if he had ever been arrested, he said he only had two minor offenses when he was a kid. My father found out later that he had been using an alias. He was using his brother's name. Turns out his real name was James and that he had been arrested numerous times."

"Yeah," Dan said. "I just learned about the brother myself, earlier this morning."

"So then you already knew."

"Yes, but thanks for calling."

"No problem."

"Oh, wait. How did your father find out he was using his brother's identity?"

"Another coworker turned him in."

"Who was it?" Dan waited for an answer, but one didn't come. "Crone? Hello?" Dan hung up the phone. "Dammit! Lost him." He put the cell back in his pocket and turned to Maday. "Did you get all that?"

"Just your side of the conversation," Maday replied.

"That was Lane Crone. He said McKinley was fired when a coworker turned him in for—" Dan paused. "It was you."

Maday lunged at Dan, grabbing for the 9mm he knew was under Dan's shirt. Dan grabbed Maday's arm with his left hand and tried for his gun with the other.

Phil caught the struggle out of the corner of his eye. "Red!" he shouted. "Do something!"

"I am doing something! I'm panicking!"

Maday got his hand around the weapon and pulled. Dan drew back and gave Maday a left to the face. Maday fell back, bringing the gun with him. He pulled the trigger and the passenger side rear window shattered.

"Holy shit!" Red hollered, taking cover behind the seat.

"What the hell is going on?" Phil hollered. "You idiots are gonna make me lose control of this crate!"

"See, I told you it was a crate," Red chimed in from his hiding place.

Dan had his fingers wrapped around the barrel of the 9mm and did his best to keep it pointed upward.

Maday pulled the trigger again, shooting a hole in the roof.

"For chrissakes!" Phil yelled. He pulled the wheel hard left sending Dan on top of Maday, the weapon between them.

The gun went off one more time and Maday relaxed.

Dan pushed away from him, the gun in *his* hand now.

A bloodstain in the middle of Maday's chest was spreading fast.

"Do you have the gun?" Phil yelled.

"Yes," Dan replied.

Maday stared at Dan. A trickle of blood ran from his mouth and dripped off his chin.

"It's almost the end of the road for you," Dan said. "Might as well fess up."

"They were having an affair," Maday said.

"Did you kill your wife?" Dan asked.

"I killed them both," McKinley said. He coughed and blood splattered on Dan's face and the front of his shirt.

Maday attempted a smile. "McKinley is under my pool."

"Where's Elizabeth, Dave?"

"I dumped her body … over the bridge near Shark Key a few months later."

"I've gotta know something, Dave," said Dan. "Why'd you want to go on this wild goose chase with me?"

Maday coughed and spluttered up blood. He was fading fast. "I knew you suspected me … I knew if I didn't play along … it would look bad."

Dave Maday coughed two more times and then stopped breathing. Dan reached over and with the tips of his fingers closed his eyelids.

"You suspected him all along?" Red asked. "Why didn't you let me in on it?"

"I, uh … I thought it would be best if I kept it to myself."

Red cocked his head. "You never suspected him, did you?"

"The important thing is, he thought I did."

"That's not really the important thing."

"I think it is."

"No."

"There's duct tape under the seat," said Phil. "Cover that hole in the roof please."

Red sighed. "Duct tape."

Chapter Thirty-Eight

It was almost seven that same evening when Dan turned the corner onto Sky View Street. As he neared Anna Tinka's house, he could see Anna carrying a cardboard box to a small U-Haul trailer she had attached to the back of her car. Sarah walked along behind her mother with a smaller box.

Sarah stopped when she saw Dan's car. He pulled to the curb across from the trailer, and got out.

"Mr. Dan!" Sarah called out.

"Hey Sarah," Dan replied. "What's going on?"

"We're moving," Sarah said, sounding both sad and excited at the same time.

"We're gonna stay with my sister for a while," Anna said. "Until we get on our feet."

"Mom's gonna get a new job," Sarah said.

"Oh yeah?" Dan said. "That's great."

"My sister's father in-law owns a big furniture store up in Homestead. She said she can get me a job there."

"I'm glad for you," Dan said. "*Both* of you."

"I'll miss you guys," said Sarah.

"We'll miss you," Dan responded. "I bet Maxine would like to say good bye. I'll run home and pick her up, and bring her back over quick so she can see you off."

"She stopped by a couple hours ago and said goodbye," Sarah said.

"Oh. Okay. I guess this is it then."

Anna closed the door of the trailer and Dan helped her with the locking mechanism.

"Thanks, Dan," Anna said.

Dan reached for his money clip. "Here, let me—"

"You've done enough," Anna said. She gave Dan a hug and a kiss on the cheek. "Say goodbye, Sarah," she said, getting into the car and starting it. "We gotta get going."

Sarah put her arms around Dan and squeezed. "Maybe I can come back down sometime and visit," she said.

"That would be great," Dan said. "You can come down anytime you like. You have mine and Maxine's phone numbers."

Sarah stepped back and wiped a little tear from the corner of her eye. "Bye." With one last smile she ran to the passenger side and got in.

Dan stood in the road and watched until they turned the corner. Then he got back into his own car and went home.

Skip was just pulling up in front of Dan's house when he got there.

"Dan the Man!" Skip shouted. He got out of the Volkswagen Thing, reached into the back seat, and pulled out a small wooden table.

Dan recognized the table right away. "What's up, Skip?" he asked.

"Brought your table back," Skip replied. He handed the repaired table to Dan.

"How did *you* end up with it?"

"Maxine gave it to me the other day. She asked if I knew anyone who could repair it. Being a dude with connections, of course, I did!"

Dan turned the table every which way as he inspected it. "Christ, you can't even tell it was broken. Thanks."

"Don't mention it, pal." Skip pulled his door open. "I gotta get going."

Dan carried the table up the steps and into the house. He set it on the floor next to Buddy's bed. He stepped back and stared at the table for a few seconds, and then went into the kitchen to heat up a cup of the morning's left-over coffee. When he returned to the dining room, he noticed the note on the table.

Dan,

I need some time. I've taken a leave of absence from work and I'm going home, to my parents' house. I'm sorry.

Maxine

"Fuck," Dan whispered. His eyes went to the bar, to the half-empty bottle of tequila. He laid the note back down on the table and walked over to the bar. He grabbed a shot glass and filled it with tequila. He glared at the glass for a moment and then picked up the bottle and chugged the entire contents. He turned and threw the bottle as hard as he could. It shattered against the case board.

The End

North Murder Beach
A Jake Stellar Novel

The first installment of the story of North Myrtle Beach police detective, Jake Stellar. The spring bike rallies have ended, the spring breakers have all gone back to school, and the summer tourist season is a few weeks away. What better time for a police officer to take a nice quiet relaxing week off from work? That's what Jake Stellar had in mind. That is until someone from his past resurfaces to remind him of a terrible secret he has spent years trying to forget. In North Murder Beach, a story of revenge, Jake is unwillingly and violently forced to confront his secret from his past.

ISBN: 978-0-9894877-1-9

The Coast of Christmas Past
From the Tales of Dan Coast

Coast of Christmas Past is the third book in the Dan Coast series of books. Dan Coast is all set to spend Christmas just the same way he has every year for the past few years; alone and drunk. But when uninvited, unexpected guests arrive and throw a wrench into his holiday plans he is forced to sober up (slightly), and throw on a smile. Just when it seems nothing else could go wrong, a close friend is injured in what appears, to the police, to be a drug deal gone bad. Dan Coast and his sidekick, Red jump into action to find the truth while their friend lies unconscious in the hospital.

ISBN: 978-0-9894877-3-3

The Man in Room Number Four
The Dunquin Cove Series

When a mysterious stranger arrives in the small coastal town of Dunquin Cove, Maine it appears as though Claire and her young son, Mica's prayers have been answer.

But who is he, and why is he really here? Join Claire and her guests at the Colsome House Bed and Breakfast as they piece together the mystery of the Man in Room Number Four.

ISBN: 978-0-9894877-2-6

Ship of Fools
From the Tales of Dan Coast

Ship of Fools is the fourth book in The Tales of Dan Coast series and begins where Coasts of Christmas Past left off. Find out how Dan deals with the death of a young friend, while looking into the disappearance of a new friend's sister. Join Dan, Red, and Skip as they fumble their way through a new mystery.

ISBN: 978-0-9894877-4-0

Beach Shoot
A Jake Stellar Series

It's a beautiful Sunday morning in North Myrtle Beach and Emily Bowen, a wife and mother of four, lies dying on the beach. Jake Stellar returns in Beach Shoot, a new mystery by Rodney Riesel.

Beach Shoot is the second Jake Stellar book and sequel to the Amazon Best Seller North Murder Beach. In Beach Shoot, Jake finds himself teamed up with the most unlikely of partners, his nemesis and fellow detective Avis Lint. Join Jake and Avis as they piece together the clues in this thrilling new mystery.

ISBN: 978-0-9894877-5-7

Return to Dunquin Cove
The Dunquin Cove Series

It's been almost six months since the day ex-hitman, Ben Dunning turned up in Dunquin Cove, Maine, not knowing where or who he was. He's lived a quiet, peaceful life in the small town, but now his old life is calling him back. As Ben plans a trip to Boston in search of his past, little does he know that trouble is brewing in Dunquin Cove. Two strangers have arrived with the promise of safety and security. Join Ben and the people of Dunquin Cove as they band together to prove they can take care of themselves and their town.

ISBN: 978-0-9894877-7-1

Double Trouble
From the Tales of Dan Coast

Shortly after Walter and Warren Bowman arrive in Key West in search of a sister they never knew they had, Warren disappears. With nowhere else to turn, Walter enlists the help of Dan Coast. Join Dan as he and sidekick Red Baxter search for the missing Bowman family members, while dealing with the fallout of an ongoing case.

ISBN: 978-0-9894877-9-5

When Death Returns
A Jake Stellar Series

Has a serial killer from the past returned to North Myrtle Beach? Jake Stellar is back in When Death Returns. Join Jake and his partner Avis Lint in this exciting third installment of the Jake Stellar series as they investigate a homicide that eerily echoes the past.

ISBN: 978-0-9971149-0-4

From Here to There: A Collection of Short Stories

Within this book is a collection of short stories I have written over the past few years. The stories were mostly inspired by trips I've taken, places I've stayed, and conversations I've overheard from Maine to Florida. Although these stories differ from ones I have released in the past, I hope you will enjoy reading them as much as I enjoyed writing them.

ISBN: 978-0-9971149-1-1

Most Likely to Die

From the Tales of Dan Coast

How does someone with no enemies end up murdered? That's for Dan Coast and his sidekick Red Baxter to find out. Join Dan and Red, along with Skip Stoner and Dan's childhood hero, former astronaut, Kip Larson as they piece together the clues that may free an innocent man. In this action packed, sixth installment of The Tales of Dan Coast Series, Dan digs into a wrongly accused man's past and finds out he may not be so innocent.

ISBN: 978-0-9971149-2-8

The Obedience of Fools
A Jake Stellar Series

Join Detective Jake Stellar and his partner, Detective Avis Lint in this fast paced, North Myrtle Beach based Jake Stellar Series. In this fourth installment, The Obedience of Fools, Jake and Avis butt heads with some of The Grand Strand's elite as they try to uncover a secret that may hold the answer to a string of recent homicides.

ISBN: 978-0-9971149-3-5

Deadly Moves
From the Tales of Dan Coast

Dan Coast has finally bought himself a new car, well, new to him. But when he returns to pick up his new ride, he gets an unwanted surprise. In Deadly Moves, the seventh installment in the Tales of Dan Coast Series, we also see the return of Officer Mel Gormin. Join Dan, Red, Mel, and Skip as they do their best to solve the murder of an elderly couple while working as bodyguards to a young starlet who is visiting Key West.

ISBN: 978-0-9971149-4-2

Sunrise City

Cole Ballinger is a retired Fort Pierce police detective and the owner of the Breakwater Bar and Grill. Cole has spent the last ten years doing his best to avoid contact with his ex-wife, but that's easier said than done when she lives in the same town and they have 3 children together. Now Cole's ex has asked for a favor: look into the violent murder of an old acquaintance.

ISBN: 978-0-9971149-6-6

Dead in the Water

When the pool boy finds the woman who hired him floating face down in her pool, he becomes the prime suspect. Dead in the Water is the fifth book in the Jake Stellar Series. In this installment, North Myrtle Beach detectives Jake Stellar and Avis Lint investigate the murder of Wanda Truman and soon find that the deeper they dig into her past, the longer the suspect list becomes.

ISBN: 978-0-9971149-7-3

www.ingramcontent.com/pod-product-compliance
Lightning Source LLC
Chambersburg PA
CBHW051947220626
47052CB00004B/832